Win!
Win!

diana noonan

PEARSON

Heinemann

Win! Win!

diana noonan

www.pearsoned.co.nz

Your comments on this book are welcome at
feedback@pearsoned.co.nz

Pearson Education New Zealand
a division of Pearson New Zealand Ltd
67 Apollo Drive, Rosedale, North Shore 0632, New Zealand

Associated companies throughout the world

© Pearson Education New Zealand 2008
First published 2008

ISBN: 978-1-86970-645-6

Produced by Pearson Education New Zealand
Commissioning Editor: Lucy Armour
Editor: Jan Chilwell
Page Layout and Design: Sarah Healey

Printed in China by Nordica

Once, when I was collecting shellfish from a remote area, the tide came in unexpectedly fast and my return route was covered with crashing waves. I was stuck. I either had to stay where I was overnight, without shelter, or return through the forest along what had once been a rough cattle track. I chose the cattle track and battled my way through the vegetation that had almost completely engulfed it during its years of disuse. I have never forgotten how proud I felt when eventually, tired, bruised and scratched, I emerged onto the road and found my car.

There is something special about being able to look after yourself in the wild. It somehow makes you a stronger, more independent person. I used this idea as the basis for *Win! Win!* but, in this novel, it is tinged with sadness. No young person Phoebe's age should be forced, by circumstances, to leave their home and care for themselves. Every young person has the right to care and protection from the people who are supposed to love them. Sometimes, they have to go to extraordinary lengths to find it.

Diana Noonan

Chapter 1

"You! Hey, you! Stop!"

Phoebe glanced back, her arm held high. Behind the reception desk a man in a dark suit was pushing his way through a swing door, panic in his eyes. Without hesitating, she threw her missile hard, then fled across the casino's thick gold and purple carpet, out onto the wet street and down the hill towards the park. She didn't even wait to see the paint hit its target.

"Stop her! Someone stop her!"

Behind her, footsteps rang out on the pavement but she was well ahead of them, dodging in and out between bewildered pedestrians.

"Stop that girl!"

An arm reached out to grab her. Phoebe tugged herself free, but her pursuer was closer now. She shot into the entrance of a car park building, sprinted towards the far wall and crouched behind a car.

She saw the man arrive. He stood at the empty ticket office, peering over the barrier arm into the darkness. Then, bent double with the effort of the chase, he pressed his mobile to his ear and staggered back out into the street.

If she went any higher in the building, Phoebe decided, she'd be trapped. All they'd have to do was block the entrance and search until they found her. Instead, she crawled behind the row of parked cars, then ducked across to the other side of the building and looked over the edge of the railing. It was just a short drop down to the alleyway below. She checked behind her, then climbed over and let herself fall.

The alleyway was narrow and littered with broken glass. Phoebe hurried along it and saw ahead the glow of flashing Christmas lights. It was the exit to the next street and, a moment later, she was walking among crowds of late-night shoppers.

She peeled off her orange jacket, hoping to be less recognisable, and walked briskly until she met the road that led to the edge of the park.

There was no one around now. She leapt a low concrete wall and ran across the grass towards the playground. She was exhausted. She wanted to rest

Win! Win!

but the thought of police dogs tracking her scent kept her moving.

Phoebe wished she knew the park better than she did. She ran through the playground and across an empty field with soccer goals at each end. The ground underfoot was sodden and water splashed up under her feet. Her chest ached with the effort of running. It hurt to breathe.

Where the field ended, she scrambled over a stile and jumped down onto a one-lane road that snaked its way through the rain towards the edge of the park. Phoebe followed the road around a corner, stopping when she saw the red tail lights of a vehicle – the rear end of a long truck. Stencilled across it were the words "Carter's Horse Transport".

A woman was coming out of a door on the side of the vehicle. If she'd looked up, she would have seen Phoebe standing in the shadows but, instead, she opened the driver's door and climbed in. The vehicle's engine rumbled into life as its headlights lit up the road.

Suddenly, Phoebe knew what she was going to do. She ran the short distance to the truck. The side door was unlocked and, as the vehicle began to lumber off, she heaved her exhausted body up the steps and pulled herself inside.

Chapter 1

It was dark and warm in the back of the truck and it smelled exactly like the stable Phoebe sometimes helped out at in the holidays. She sat down on the floor as the vehicle began to bump along the road and, from somewhere towards the front of the truck, a horse whinnied and stamped its feet. Another animal gave a throaty rumble in reply. They were comforting noises and, for the moment anyway, they made Phoebe feel safe.

She breathed in the dusty smell of straw and felt the beat of her heart begin to lose its rapid pace. She leaned against the side of the truck, unzipped the pocket of her jacket and reached inside.

"Alfie!" she whispered to the soft little creature that sniffed her hand. "Are you all right?"

Gently, she ran her fingers along Alfie's tail. Then she stroked his soft tummy.

"Come on. Out you come. You had a bumpy ride, didn't you?"

She scooped up the little white rat and drew him out of her pocket.

"There you are. It's all right. We're safe now."

She held Alfie up to her face and rubbed her cheek against his sleek coat.

"We're in trouble, Alfie," she whispered into the darkness. "I've done something terrible."

Alfie slipped out of her hand and crept up to the neck of her T-shirt. He nosed his way under her hair and rested there, snug and warm against her skin.

Phoebe let out a long, shaky sigh. She *had* done something terrible, and now she was in a truck and had no idea where she was going.

"Just away," she whispered to herself.

Away from Mum, and away from the police who, by now, would be looking for her. But, most of all, away from Mick.

The truck's brakes hissed and the vehicle slowed a little before lumbering off once more.

Phoebe couldn't remember when Mick had first started gambling. When Mum had met him, Phoebe was ten. Mick had been working for an advertising business. Sometimes, in the weekend, he would take them to the races.

Phoebe had never been to the horse races before. She didn't care about the races so much. It was the horses she liked. They were handsome and strong and when they ran like the wind their beautiful tails trailed out behind them like wild streamers. She hadn't liked it when their jockeys lashed at them with whips or when the horses sweated and foamed at the mouth when the race was over.

Mick was mad on the races. He knew the names

of all the horses and what they'd won at other race meetings. He said that some horses were "pure gold" and he was always telling Mum which ones to bet on. He said he had tips from people who knew.

Mum was teacher-aiding then. Her money was her own and she didn't like spending it. "It has to last me," she'd tell Mick and he'd laugh and ask how she ever expected to make money if she wasn't prepared to spend it.

Phoebe reached up and stroked Alfie. At the same time, the truck braked and a glow of red shone in through the window at the top of the side door. Phoebe pulled herself up and looked out. They were at a traffic intersection. There were cars everywhere. The roads were crazy. Not surprising since it was nine o'clock on a Friday night and Christmas was only four days away.

It felt strange to have no idea where she was heading and no plans about what to do next. But, right now, all she cared about was escaping from the police – that and never having to see Mick again. She bit her lip hard and ran her fingers down Alfie's sleek tail. If Mum chose to stay with Mick, then she couldn't have Phoebe as well.

Alfie squirmed and snuggled more deeply into Phoebe's hair.

Win! Win!

"I've got you, little rat," she said, gently scratching behind his paper-thin ears. "We've got each other."

The truck began to move again. In the half-darkness, Phoebe looked around the vehicle. There were several empty stalls. In fact, only the three at the front of the truck contained animals. Draped over the sides of two of the stalls were horse blankets – heavy, rough canvas things, but with soft woollen linings. Phoebe felt tired, drained of energy. It would be so good to sleep.

She reached up and hauled one of the covers down to the floor. Then she scooped Alfie up and slipped him into the zip pocket of her jacket.

"We don't want you wandering around when I'm asleep," she told him.

She lay down, reassuring herself that, if the truck stopped again, she would hear the change of noise from the engine and wake up. If the driver came in to check on the horses, Phoebe would climb under the cover.

She closed her eyes. At home, Mum would be wondering where Phoebe was. She'd said that she was going to Sreya's and would be back by nine. If she'd had her mobile, she could have phoned to tell Mum that she was okay, that she was just going away for a while. But Mick had nicked her

phone weeks ago, when the money on his own had run out.

Phoebe's stomach tightened into a hard knot. She couldn't stay at home any more, not with Mick there, lying, cheating, threatening. And, after what she'd done tonight, she couldn't go back even if she wanted to because, before long, the police would be there, waiting to take her away.

Phoebe hated Mick and she hated the way Mum was so fooled by him, so weak. But, no matter what he did, no matter how much he took from them, Phoebe was sure that Mum would never leave him.

"He'll take Jak," Mum had said to Phoebe the last time they'd talked about it. "If I leave him, he'll go for custody and he'll take Jak away from us."

Phoebe knew that wasn't true. Mick wasn't interested in baby Jak. He wasn't interested in anything except his next visit to the casino. Mum was the problem. It was as though she didn't know how to manage on her own any more, even though she'd done it for years after she and Dad had split up. It was as though she was joined to Mick by some horrible, invisible glue and couldn't see that he would never, ever be any different.

What was worse, what was far worse than that,

was that Mum didn't seem to see Phoebe any more. She didn't see that she needed everyday things like clothes and school stuff, even food. Sometimes, it was as though Mum couldn't even see that Phoebe needed *her*. There was nothing left of Mum for anyone but Mick.

Phoebe yawned. She was too tired to think any more. Her head hurt and all she wanted to do was sleep. She breathed in the smell of straw and animals. It was warm in the truck, warm and safe, and the thrum of the vehicle's engine was like a distant song.

Chapter 1

Chapter 2

"Nick, are you *still* on the computer? It's almost ten o'clock."

"It's Friday night, Mum. *And* it's holidays."

"I know," said Julia, "but all the same, it's getting late."

"Just about finished."

"Who are you talking to?"

"Sean."

"Tell him to say hello to his mum for me."

Nick sighed. Mum was always doing that. Sending messages to his friends' mothers.

The alert chime drew Nick's attention back to the screen. Sean's display picture, a fish, flashed up in the top right of the window and Nick clicked on it.

"Whn R U leavin 4 da beach?" he read.

"Sunday," he typed back. "How bout U guys?"

"Same," Sean replied. "Bring hooks + sinkers."

"+ nails 2 finish hut," typed Nick.

"Got an idea 4 da raft," came Sean's reply.

"Nick!" called Mum. "Bed!"

"GTG," typed Nick hastily. "C U Sunday."

In his room, Nick tugged off his jeans and climbed into bed, but he knew he'd never sleep. Just one more day to go and then he and Mum and Dad and his sisters would be in the car and heading south to the beach house at Spratten.

Nick couldn't remember a time when his family hadn't gone to Spratten for the Christmas holidays. And, since Sean and his family had been coming to stay in Sean's uncle's place, it was even better.

Julia arrived at the door and looked down at the floor.

"You're wearing your clothes, aren't you?" she asked flatly.

Nick smirked. "Not my jeans."

"What do you think PJs are for?" said Julia. She picked up his pyjamas and biffed them at him. "Grub!" she said with a grin.

"Hey, Mum," began Nick, "do you think it's weird that Sean's my best friend when he lives so far away from us and we only see each other a couple of times a year?"

"Friendship's not about distance," said Julia.

"But it's, like, when we meet up at the beach, nothing's changed. It's just, like, 'Hi!' and then we're doing stuff together."

"Nick?" Nick's dad, Tom, came into the room. "What are you two talking about?" he asked.

"Love," said Julia.

"No we're not," said Nick. "We were talking about friends."

"It's all the same," said Julia. "Love, friendship . . . It's what holds the world together." She waved a hand in the air and walked out the door. "Night, night."

Dad rolled his eyes at Nick in sympathy. Mum was always talking about that sort of stuff. Dad said it was because she was a social worker and, in her job, love was often in short supply.

"Hey," said Tom, changing the subject, "I've been thinking about the Spratten triathlon and the raft race section."

He sat down on the end of Nick's bed. His eyes were sparkling. Sometimes, thought Nick, Dad loved being down at the beach more than anyone else.

"We have to build the raft ourselves," said Nick. "That's the rules. Kids have to make and paddle their raft themselves."

Win! Win!

"I know, but parents can give some *ideas*, can't they?"

Nick felt sorry for Dad. He was like a little kid when it came to competitions and building stuff.

"I guess so," he said. "But I've just been talking to Sean and he says he's got some ideas of his own."

"If we could get hold of some of those really big inner tubes – the sort that trucks use," continued Tom, "and a tarpaulin, we . . . I mean you and Sean could wrap it round the tubes. Then, if you constructed a light deck to go on top, maybe plywood or something . . ."

Nick nodded. "But we have to do it ourselves, Dad."

Tom held up his hands. "Absolutely! No way round that. I'm just here for advice." He moved onto his favourite subject. "Got your fishing gear organised?"

"I oiled my reel last night," said Nick. "I think I'm going to need some fresh gut though. The stuff I've got is pretty rotten."

"I'll mend the gear when we're down there," said Tom.

"How long have you been going to the beach house?" asked Nick. He knew the answer but he wanted to hear it again.

"Since before I was your age," replied Tom. He looked at the clock beside Nick's bed. "Look at the time! Got to get some sleep. Big day ahead tomorrow with all the packing we've got to do."

Nick heard him whistling as he went down the hall. Christmas holidays were great. He snuggled down in his bed and switched off his light.

Sean closed down the computer. Just two more nights to go and then, on Sunday morning, he'd be at the beach, staying in his uncle's fishing hut at Spratten, overlooking the estuary. He could almost smell the smoke from the hut's coal range and the kerosene fumes from the lamps that were used to light the place at night. There was no electricity at their hut, no TV, no phone, no computer. Just the sound of the tide rippling in over the wet sand, the crash of breakers on the bar and, at night, the water birds squabbling on the little sandy islands on the other side of the estuary. All that and Nick, too, just four doors down. At low tide they could walk along the sand to visit each other.

Win! Win!

Sean was still sitting at the computer desk, thinking about it, when his mum, Marie, called out to him.

"I'm away now, Sean. Don't forget to lock the door after me."

"Okay," he called back.

"Take the phone to bed with you," she said, coming along the hall to say goodnight. "I don't think Fin's going to wake up. He had a big day at kindy."

"Night, Mum," said Sean.

Marie went out, closing the door quietly behind her, and Sean heard the car reversing down the drive. He and Fin weren't supposed to be at home on their own, not when Sean was only thirteen. But Mum didn't have much choice if they were going to have the things that other people had, like a computer – and holidays. You couldn't have that sort of stuff if you had to pay for a babysitter.

Uncle Luke, Mum's brother, let them stay in the hut at Spratten for nothing but they still had to find the money for the petrol to get there. So, three times a week, Mum cleaned at the car factory after the late shift finished. She got home at two in the morning and then was up at eight the next morning to get Sean's breakfast and make his school lunch.

Chapter 2

15

Sean thought about the hut again. Mum slept on the sofa in the little kitchen when they were there and, some mornings, Sean would get up before her and light the stove and cook toast on the top. He'd make tea and then grab his sleeping bag and squeeze in beside her on the sofa. They'd have breakfast in bed, talking together before Fin woke, while they waited for the room to warm up.

Mum would tell him about the holidays she'd had when she was a kid and Sean would tell her about school and what he did with his friends and all the stuff that they never seemed to get time to talk about at home. Sometimes, Mum wanted to talk about Dad. It wasn't so much that she wanted to talk *about* him, it was more that she wanted to make sure that Sean understood that she'd done the right thing by telling Dad he had to leave. Sean didn't want to think about that. It felt too much like he was taking sides.

At the door to Fin's room, he poked his head in and checked that his little brother was okay. He was sleeping on his front, like two-year-olds always did, and his soft toys were taking up most of the space in his bed.

Fin loved being at Spratten, too – making sand

pies on the edge of the estuary and dangling a little hand line off the end of the wharf. Nick's big sisters loved him. They were always taking him away to their place to play or wheeling him along the sand in his baby buggy.

"Spratten," said Sean softly to himself as he went into his room. He couldn't wait to get there. There was absolutely nowhere better to be for the holidays than the beach, and hanging out with Nick.

He sat down on his bed and kicked off his shoes. The only thing that could go wrong was if Dad decided to come down, uninvited, for a visit. But he wouldn't do that because Mum had told him they were going to Gran's for Christmas and, besides, there was that police protection order thing that said he couldn't.

Sean reached out for the Christmas card on the drawers beside his bed. "Hope you have a great Christmas, mate," said the writing inside. "Love you heaps, Dad." He was still holding the card when his mobile buzzed into life.

"Seanie?" said the voice on the other end of the line.

"Dad?"

"Is Mum at work?"

Sean hesitated. "Yeah."

"So," said Dad. "What are you up to? Going anywhere special for Christmas?"

Win! Win!

Chapter 3

When Phoebe woke, it was 1am. She had been asleep for three hours and it was now completely dark in the back of the truck. The vehicle was still moving and, when she stood up and looked through the window in the door, there was nothing to see except the lights of occasional vehicles passing in the opposite direction.

The truck was on the open road and moving fast, but Phoebe had no idea what direction it had travelled in when it left the city. She swallowed hard to suppress the sudden panic she felt at being trapped inside.

The back of the truck was no longer as fresh as it had been when she first climbed in. The air smelled of horse sweat and manure and it was uncomfortably warm. She reached for her jacket and felt in the pocket for Alfie. He was usually most active at night, but for now he seemed content to stay where he was. She flopped back down on the horse cover. Her eyelids felt heavy.

It was the sound of voices that woke her for the second time that night – that and the absence of the throb from the engine. A yellow light penetrated the dimness in the back of the truck and there were footsteps getting louder outside. She scrambled under the horse cover as the door opened.

"How many you got on board?" asked a man's deep voice.

"Three," replied the driver. "Couple of racers going down for training and a kid's pony."

"How far did you say you were going?"

"Quarry Flat."

"Quarry *Flat*?"

"Just south of Martindale. You leave the main road at the junction to the coast and take the inland route."

Phoebe could barely breathe under the thick cover.

"Another three hours then. Want water for them?"

"Na, they never drink when they're being floated."

The door banged shut and Phoebe heard a familiar sound. The truck was being refuelled. She waited until the engine bumped into life then peeped

Win! Win!

through the window. The name of the garage gave no clue as to where they were. She also had no idea where Martindale was.

She lay down again and tried some calculations in her head. A truck probably travelled a little more slowly than a car – say ninety kilometres an hour? And she'd been asleep for three hours. So she was around two hundred and seventy kilometres from home.

She sat up and leaned against one of the stalls. Mum would be out of her mind worrying about her. Maybe she'd even called the police. Maybe they'd put two and two together and realised that she was the girl who had run from the casino after . . . but Phoebe couldn't let her mind go any further in that direction.

Alfie didn't want to be stroked. He was washing himself inside her pocket. Phoebe realised that she had no water for him – and none for herself, for that matter, or food.

She let her mind wander and thought about baby Jak. He'd miss her. He was eight months old and teething – always poking his fists into his mouth and chewing them.

He looked like Mick. Even Phoebe could see that. Stupid, stupid Mum. Just when things were worse

than ever, when Mick had gone from race horses to the casino. Just when it looked as though Mum might finally leave him, she'd got pregnant, and so ill with morning sickness that she'd had to give up her teacher-aid job. Mick's salary was all they had, and what was left of that after he'd gambled it away was just a laugh.

Phoebe picked up a piece of straw and chewed on it. Though she didn't really feel tired, she found her eyes beginning to close again.

At around 3.30am, Alfie started butting the inside of the jacket pocket and the movement against her leg woke her. If she didn't take him out, he'd chew a hole through the fabric. But, just as she went to unzip the pocket, the truck's brakes hissed and the vehicle slowed to a crawl, then stopped with its engine still running.

Phoebe looked out and saw a cluster of road signs lit up in the headlights. "Martindale 53 kilometres," said one, pointing back the way they had come. "Coastal Highway Scenic Route," she read on another.

The truck was about to turn off. She could see the flashing orange glow from its indicator light at the rear of the vehicle. It was still dark but sunrise would be just a couple of hours away.

Win! Win!

If she left the vehicle now, she wouldn't be seen.

It was a split-second decision. Phoebe reached for the door handle as the engine revved and, the next minute, she had jumped and was sliding down a steep ditch and into long grass.

She waited where she was until the truck had made its turn and the driver had climbed out to attend to the banging door that Phoebe had left open. Then the vehicle drove away and the night was still except for the shrill whistle of frogs.

She was in the country and the road she was on (the road that led to the coast) was unsealed. A forest of tall trees lined the route and, up above, the sky was filled with stars.

After about an hour of walking, she arrived at a bridge and navigated her way by moonlight down a short bank to a trickle of a stream. She drank from it, scooping up water in her hands for herself and Alfie. Then she was back on the road.

Just before five, she reached the top of a steep hill where the trees gave way to pasture and grazing cattle. In front of her, dimly visible in the first pale flicker of dawn, was the ocean, its grey waves crashing on the beach of a long bay.

By the time she had descended the hill, the sun was rising above the cliffs at the far end of the bay.

A small settlement – no more than a ragged jumble of twenty or thirty houses – was coming into view, hugging the edge of a wide river estuary.

Phoebe was very hungry. Where there were houses, she thought, there was likely to be food, perhaps even a shop – not that she had any money with her. At the edge of the settlement – it was too early for anyone to be up – a sign showing a couple of children fishing read, "Welcome to Spratten".

Most of the buildings were just huts that had been joined together to make small beach houses, but they were well painted and most of the grass around them was mowed. The curtains in every window were pulled and there were no cars in the driveways. It was a holiday place, Phoebe decided. Christmas was still three days away and the families that came here hadn't yet arrived.

Her stomach rumbled. She looked up and down the road and then let herself in through one of the gates. When she tried the door of a house, she found it firmly locked.

She did the same at another place, and another. She'd stopped to check once more that there was no one about when she noticed vegetables growing in a section that looked more cared for than the others.

Even if someone lived there permanently, thought Phoebe, they wouldn't be awake yet. She was so hungry she was prepared to take the risk of going into the garden.

She climbed a couple of fences and crouched behind a row of broad, green leaves. She picked some and then discovered courgettes lying on the ground. There were carrots, too, and some lettuce and broccoli. It was too scary to eat where she was, so she gathered as much as she could and shot down to the back of the section, where lupins and sand dunes led down to the estuary. It was horrible having to steal, but what choice did she have?

When Phoebe offered Alfie some broccoli, he took it in his paws and nibbled it, hollowing out the stalk and dropping the tough outer skin onto Phoebe's shoulder. She washed the carrots in the river and crunched on them. She was still hungry when she finished but, when she crept up the dunes to the bottom of the section, a light was on in the house and the curtains were slightly parted.

It was no longer safe to be wandering around the village, not if people were awake. But, while there was the possibility of finding more food, she couldn't afford to leave the settlement yet. The answer was to hide somewhere until it was dark

and then make another raid on the garden, and any others she could find.

At the seaward end of the village, the dunes ran back to meet forest. That was the place to be. She would sleep in the undergrowth and wait until night.

She set off along the edge of the river, hugging the base of the dunes so that anyone looking out from their beach house wouldn't be able to see her.

"Hold tight, Alfie," she warned as she leapt a stream that ran across the sand to join the river.

Level with the river mouth, she pushed through a stretch of marram grass and struggled over clumps of low-growing ferns that gave way to true forest. Trailing vines with prickly leaves tugged at her clothes. For a while it was difficult to make any progress, but she soon found herself on a rough track and, after walking for several minutes, she came to a clearing beneath a huge tree. A knotted rope hung from its upper branches and someone had constructed a rough wooden ladder that led up to a platform made of boards.

Phoebe hauled herself up the rungs and, at the top, pushed open a hinged flap in the floor. She was in a hut with board walls and an iron roof. In one corner sat a small tin trunk fastened with a tiny padlock.

Win! Win!

Chapter 4

It was Sunday morning. "Right, everyone out to the car!" ordered Tom.

Nick scanned his room, looking for anything important that he'd forgotten to pack.

"Too late for that," said Tom, following his gaze. "Can't fit anything else on the trailer."

"If Jess and Kirsty weren't taking so many clothes, we'd be able to fit in a tonne more," grumbled Nick.

Sisters! And, as for Mum, she'd packed a whole library. How many books could you read in ten days!

"Where are my hair tongs?" wailed Kirsty.

"I chucked them in with my stuff," said Jess.

Nick's sisters were just eighteen months apart and they looked like twins. During the year, when they were away from home at university, he kind of missed them. But, when they came home for the summer, they drove him crazy.

"Out! Everybody out of the house!" demanded Tom. "I'm locking up."

Julia was already in the car, calm and collected as usual, a book open on her lap. Nick got into the back seat and took out his mobile as the girls squashed in on either side of him. They stank of hair product and deodorant.

He couldn't wait to get to the beach and get the smell of fish under his fingernails.

"Who are you texting?" demanded Kirsty.

"Sean," said Nick. "And don't look over my shoulder."

"Touchy, touchy," said Jess, taking out her own mobile.

"You won't be able to use those for much longer," said Kirsty. "It's a pain having no coverage down at the beach."

"Poor Marie," said Julia from the front seat. "She's had to do all her packing on her own."

Nick paused in his texting and looked up. Mum was always worrying about Sean's mum.

"Still, at least she doesn't have that wretched husband to worry about any more."

Nick felt uncomfortable. That was Sean's dad she was talking about. Nick didn't know exactly what it was that was so wrong with him because Mum

Win! Win!

would never give him any details, and Sean didn't talk about it.

He went back to his texting.

A hundred kilometres away, Sean's phone vibrated in his pocket.

"Where R U?" said the message.

"Who's that?" asked Marie. "Nick?"

"Yep. They're just leaving."

Marie looked into the rear-view mirror of their old wagon. "What's Fin up to?"

"He's asleep," said Sean.

In his car seat, Finny was like an island in the middle of all the vegetables that Marie had picked from their garden before they'd left home.

"Well, I'm not leaving them to go to waste," she'd said. "And besides, we can't afford to pay the prices the camp shop wants for fresh vegies."

That was typical of Mum, thought Sean – always planning ahead, saving here and there, not wasting a cent. She was such a good manager, always doing everything she could to make sure that Fin and he had what they needed, always doing what was best

for them. Which was why Sean felt so terrible. He'd let her down, big time, and he didn't know what to do about it.

He hadn't meant to, but it was so hard. Dad had just come straight out with it. "Where are you going for Christmas?" he'd asked and there was no time to make anything up.

"I thought Mum told you?" Sean had hedged, but Dad was too smart for that.

"Where are you *really* going?" he'd wanted to know and, when Sean said he couldn't say, Dad had said, "So, don't you want to see me at Christmas?"

Sean had got really confused then, and Dad had said that it was all right now, he'd changed, he was different. He had a job and his own flat and everything. He just wanted to see Sean – and Fin – at Christmas.

"We're just south of Martindale," texted Sean to Nick.

"You'll B there hrs B 4 us," replied Nick. "Don't forget the hut rule."

"You're doing an awful lot of texting, aren't you?" asked Marie.

"It only costs a few cents," Sean told her.

"It all adds up."

Sean wanted to tell her what Dad had said – that

Win! Win!

he had fifty dollars worth of phone cards that he was going to give him when he came down to the beach. But he couldn't even say that they'd been speaking, because Dad wasn't supposed to call him on his mobile, and only on the landline after tea between 6 and 7pm, when Mum was home. Dad had said he'd get into trouble with the police if Sean told Mum he'd called when she was out.

"GTG," he texted Nick and put his phone away in his pocket.

Sean stared out the window. The farm land was starting to change to patches of native forest where the trees hadn't been cleared from the steepest slopes. There were fewer sheep and more cattle – big ginger-orange beasts munching on tufts of grass with saliva drooling from their mouths.

"This is it," said Marie, braking carefully for the turn-off so that Fin wasn't disturbed. "Only eleven more kilometres to go."

As the wagon turned onto the gravel road, Sean wound up his window to keep out the dust. The car rattled and shook as though it was going to fall to bits, but Marie didn't flinch. She was really proud of the old bomb. "We don't owe a cent on it and it's all our own," she told everyone.

"I can't wait," she said suddenly. "Sun and sand –

you bringing home a fish every day. It's going to be a great holiday."

She smiled and looked across at Sean and he tried to smile back.

At the edge of the sand dunes, Phoebe stood looking out to sea. She'd woken early, though "woken" wasn't quite right, considering she'd been so cold and uncomfortable lying on the hard floor of the hut that she'd only really dozed during the long night.

She rummaged around in her tired mind for dates and details, but it seemed so long ago that she'd hopped into the back of the horse truck. Today was Sunday, she knew that much. She'd arrived in Spratten on Saturday morning, before anyone was awake. Finding the hut in the trees had been a lucky break. Finding food in the tin trunk was even more amazing.

It hadn't taken much to break open the catch. It was fastened with one of those tiny little padlocks that come in Christmas crackers. One bash with a rock and it sprang open. And inside was the food –

Win! Win!

three cans of baked beans and one of pineapple.

The bean cans had tear-tab lids so she'd eaten half of one immediately and then taken the rest deeper into the bush. Not so deep that she couldn't hear the sound of the sea though, because she didn't want to get lost. She'd found a clearing under a huge tree that was shedding its rust-brown bark on the ground. A little way off she'd discovered a tiny brown stream where she could get a drink.

Alfie had liked the beans. He'd held each one individually in his pink, silky paws, turning them over and over before hollowing out the centres. Then he'd sat on Phoebe's knee, cleaning the tomato sauce off his whiskers and stopping occasionally to stand bolt upright on his hind legs, sniffing the air suspiciously.

Did he smell wild rats? Phoebe wondered.

She and Alfie had returned to the tree hut on Saturday evening, eaten another tin of beans, and smashed open enough of the tin of pineapple with a rock to suck out the juice. Then Phoebe had somehow managed to doze on the hard floor.

Now, standing among the wild yellow lupins, it occurred to her that she must think of the future, make plans. Perhaps, she thought briefly, watching the breakers crash onto the beach, she should

consider facing the consequences of what she had done at the High Tower Casino on Friday night.

She stared into space, trying to imagine what it would be like to live in a home for kids who broke the law. Would they let her keep Alfie there? She took him out of her pocket and, for the first time since she'd left home, her eyes filled with tears. She didn't want to be without him. She stroked his back and scratched gently behind his ears. She loved him and he loved her. He depended on her.

Phoebe sniffed hard and rubbed her eyes. She couldn't afford to get miserable, not when she had to look after herself – and Alfie. She had to think about where their next meal was coming from and where they were going to sleep. She held him close. When you loved something – or someone – you thought about those sorts of things

She took a deep, shuddery breath. If Mum had loved her, *really* loved her, she'd have found a way to make things better. But she hadn't. She'd chosen Mick instead and it was as though Phoebe and baby Jak didn't even count.

She looked along the beach towards the houses. Smoke was coming from one of the chimneys. She was pretty sure it was the place where she'd stolen the vegetables. With people about, there was no way

Win! Win!

she could afford to look around the village – not until it got dark.

She popped Alfie into her pocket and turned back towards the forest. She'd spend the rest of the day in the clearing, but first she'd go back to the hut and collect the other can of beans and the half-opened tin of pineapple.

Chapter 5

"Here at last," said Marie, opening the door of the car. "Ten o'clock, not bad going." She stretched her arms above her head. "Just smell that sea!"

"I'll open up," Sean announced, bounding across the grass and long clover to the door of the little beach house.

It was all exactly as he remembered – the peeling paint on the outside, the bucket over the chimney, a pile of driftwood kindling under the front deck and the fishing buoys hanging from a hook on the outside wall. His stomach tingled with the excitement of it.

He opened up the main door first and peered inside.

"Looks like the rats have been in," he called back to Marie.

"Can't be helped," she replied. "They'll soon move out when they hear we've come to stay."

Sean picked up a few pieces of chewed paper and tossed them into the bucket beside the coal range. Then he found the ladder under the house and climbed onto the roof to take the bucket off the chimney.

"I'll get the fire going," he said, coming down again. "I'll just open up the shed and find the axe."

Marie opened the boot and started carrying boxes and bags into the hut. By the time Fin woke, crying to be taken out of his car seat, the fire was set. Sean struck a match to light the paper and blew on the flames to spread them across the kindling. He filled the kettle and placed it on top of the stove, then set up the fireguard to keep Fin from getting too close to the heat.

"Want me to take him for a walk while you unpack?" asked Sean, as Fin wriggled and grizzled under Mum's arm.

"That would be great," said Marie, giving him a hug. "You're fantastic. You know exactly how to help. I'll just find a banana for Finny and you can take him away in the baby pack for half an hour."

Sean felt so guilty he almost blurted out then and there about the phone conversation with Dad. But Mum was so happy to be at the beach house that he couldn't tell her. He just couldn't.

"Ready?" he asked Fin, once they'd both had something to eat. "Sean's going to take you to the beach."

Fin gave a squeal of anticipation as Sean lifted him into his pack and hoisted it onto his back.

Down on the sand, they headed straight for the river mouth. Sean knew there was no hope that Nick was at his place yet, but he looked up at the house anyway. It was bigger than most of the other beach houses, with four bedrooms and a couple of bathrooms. Nick's parents had heaps of money. His dad was a vet and his mum did something to help families that were in trouble.

"They don't act like they're any different though," Marie always told Sean. "They're so . . . so *nice*. Just ordinary really."

Sean smiled to himself. Mum always described people as "ordinary" when she really liked them.

At the river mouth, Sean cut across the marram grass, heading for the forest. Someone had been there before him. There were fresh footprints in the sand and the grass had been flattened. He followed the trail, pushing through the low ferns until he was in the forest. A bird flitted past and Fin pointed to it excitedly.

"We're going to see Nick and Sean's hut," said

Win! Win!

Sean. "When you're a big boy, you can climb up into it, too."

Sean followed the blazes on the trees that indicated he was on the right track and, a moment later, the hut came into sight.

"There it is!" he told Finny. "It's still up there. The wind hasn't blown it down."

Phoebe was in the hut, reaching for the cans of food, when she heard voices. They were coming from the direction of the beach and they were growing louder. She closed the trapdoor in the floor and sat completely still. A couple of minutes later, the whole hut shook.

"Strong as ever," said Sean, rattling the ladder.

"Bird!" said Fin, as something swooped past them.

"You and your birds," said Sean, laughing. "That's a wood pigeon."

Phoebe moved very slightly so that she was looking through a small crack between two boards. Below, a boy was standing at the base of the tree. He had roughly cut dark hair pulled back into a skinny

ponytail. He looked about thirteen or fourteen years old. In a pack on his back he was carrying a little boy with a chubby face and a yellow sunhat.

The older boy shook the ladder again.

"Can't go up there yet though," said Sean. "That's the rules, Fin. We have to wait until Nick arrives. Then we'll go up to the hut together."

Phoebe kept perfectly still. It seemed to take forever before the boy turned back towards the beach and, even then, he kept stopping to glance back up at the hut.

As soon as he was out of sight, she lifted the lid on the tin trunk. She would take everything that was in there – the last of the beans, the pineapple, matches, a few sheets of paper, a candle. There was no way she could risk returning, not now that the boy was planning to come back. She scooped Alfie up and set him on her shoulder. Then she tied everything into her jacket, climbed down the ladder and headed for the clearing beneath the big tree.

By the time Phoebe had eaten the beans and drained the juice from the tin of pineapple, which she had still not managed to open, the sun was high in the sky. She stuffed the candle, matches and paper into one of her pockets, and Alfie into the other, and ventured onto the beach.

Win! Win!

It was almost busy with people. Two family groups were paddling though the shallow water at the edge of the estuary and a couple was strolling along the beach, hand in hand. At last it felt less risky to be seen. She was just a holiday-maker like everyone else and soon, when a few more houses had filled up, no one would notice her.

She lay in the dunes, enjoying the warmth of the sun and catching up on lost sleep. When she woke, it was mid-afternoon and the tide was further out. She headed to where the sand ended, half a kilometre away, at a low shelf of rock that jutted into the sea. A vehicle was parked there and, when Phoebe reached it, she found a father and son on the other side of it, sheltering out of the wind. They had built a small fire; balanced over it was a metal baking tray piled high with mussels.

"Good day for it," said the man, smiling at Phoebe.

She smiled back and looked at the shellfish. They were spilling juice onto the tray and they smelled delicious.

"Did you get those around here?" she asked, as casually as she could.

"Just off the rocks," said the man, pointing with the blade of his pocket knife. "Hard work though.

Got to get them right on low tide."

Phoebe looked at the sea. "Is it low tide now?"

"It turned about half an hour ago."

"You'd still get mussels on Green Point for another hour if you hurried," said the boy.

"Where's Green Point?"

"Further round the rocks. If you go now, you can get there along the sand. It'd take, maybe . . ." He looked at his father.

"Fifteen minutes?" guessed the man. He paused. "Are you going on your own?"

Phoebe nodded.

"Well, just watch the tide," he cautioned. "You've got a long trek home if you can't get back along the sand."

The aroma of the cooking mussels was making her hungry.

"Thanks," she said, already beginning to jog away. "Thanks very much."

The rocks were rough and covered in limpets. Phoebe bounded across them and jumped narrow channels of water lined with dark-purple anemones marooned by the low tide. In one deep pool she saw an orange starfish draped lazily over a rock.

Then she was on the sand again – a narrow stretch fringed by boulders. Behind them, reeds sprouted in

  Win! Win!

clumps where a slimy brown stream snaked its way over the beach. Tall forest, a dark jungle of trees and vines, formed a dense backdrop to it all.

A little way on, the hills behind the beach grew higher so that, in places, Phoebe could see steep outcrops of grey rock that formed bluffs peeping through the forest. Gnarled trees with black bark and bright red flowers grew from the crevices in the bluffs and lit up the green world like Christmas decorations.

How many days *was* it until Christmas? She couldn't remember. She was beginning to lose track of time.

Around the next bend in the beach, she saw what had to be Green Point. It was a long platform of dark rock that stretched into the sea, its farthest point covered in thick brown kelp that shimmered in the sun. No one else was around.

When she reached it, she took off her jacket and left it lying on the beach under a rock where Alfie would be sheltered from the heat. Then she ran towards the point. Getting out there was surprisingly difficult. There were places where the water crossed the platform, leaving wide pools, so that Phoebe had to take off her shoes and socks and roll up the legs of her jeans to wade. Barnacles tore at the soles

of her feet and, when she padded gingerly over the rock, she saw that she was leaving behind patches of blood on the stone.

The rock platform narrowed towards the point and breakers crashed against its rock walls and spilled across its tip. It was too sharp underfoot to walk in bare feet, so she tugged on her shoes and laced them up again.

When she reached the end of the platform, she was disappointed to find there were no mussels to be seen. Guessing that they were hiding beneath the kelp, she got down on her hands and knees and began a cautious crawl over the rock. She wished that the sea sounded less fierce and that the waves would stop soaking her with spray. If only she could turn back but, by now, she was *very* hungry – and the mussels had to be here somewhere.

Chapter 6

"Where'd you go?" asked Marie. "You were ages."

"Checked out the hut," Sean told her. He lifted the baby pack off his shoulders and set it down on the floor. "He's almost getting too big for that thing."

"I know," said Marie. "You're a big boy, aren't you, Fin?" She picked him up and gave him a cuddle.

"We went down to the shop, too," Sean told her. "I got Fin and me some pineapple chunks." He looked up at Marie. "Was that okay?"

"Of course," she said. "You've got your holiday money from Gran. But just remember, when it runs out, it runs out. I don't have any more to give you."

"I know."

"Did you check out the camp?"

"Yep. It's starting to fill up. A few caravans and a couple of tents."

"I've put up the Christmas cards," said Marie.

"We need to get a tree to put the presents under."

Sean looked at the row of bright cards hanging over a string above the mantelpiece.

"I'm sorry you didn't get one from Dad," she said. "Fin's too little to care, but I know you do."

"I did get one from him," said Sean.

Marie looked up sharply. "You didn't tell me."

"It came in the mail. He didn't bring it round or anything."

"Okay," said Marie, nodding slowly, "but you should let me know that sort of stuff."

"It was only a card."

"All the same . . ."

Sean didn't like the way Mum looked hurt and worried at the same time.

"I'll go and get us a tree," he said, trying to change the subject, but Marie wasn't finished.

"I know it's hard," she said, sitting down on the couch behind Fin. "But it's the only way."

Sean didn't want to talk about Dad. "I'll ask Mr Somerville if I can get a bit off the pine tree at the back of his house," he said. "I saw their car pull up when Fin and I were coming back."

"You do that then," said Marie with a smile. "Take the saw from the shed – and be careful up that tree!"

Win! Win!

When the first wave sloshed over her, Phoebe was knocked backwards. The kelp cushioned her fall, but she was terrified that she'd be sucked back into the sea. She held fast to some kelp as the water swished past her, tugging at her legs.

It had been a freak wave, coming out of nowhere, and now she was drenched. Phoebe crawled back from the tip of the point and looked anxiously towards the beach, but Alfie was all right. Her jacket was well out of reach of the water.

If there had been a choice, she would have given up the search for the mussels, but now she was starving, desperate for something to eat, and there was nothing else. She'd have to watch the sea more carefully though. She couldn't risk being caught by another wave like the last big one. She might not be so lucky next time.

She began her crawl across the kelp once more, but this time she kept an eye on the sea. Further and further out she crept, pushing back the seaweed as she went. It was exhausting and she felt weak with hunger. Mussels couldn't be so hard to find. Where *were* they?

And then she saw them – the thin, rounded ends of their blue-black shells pointing straight up at her. There were dozens of them, whole nests poking out of the briny crevices. She glanced up to check for waves and reached down. How was she going to get a grip on them? They were packed so tightly together.

Phoebe pulled at one, but her fingers slid off it. She tried another and winced as a barnacle ripped at her skin and blood from the cut stained the water. Determined to succeed, she tugged and twisted at one of the shells and almost fell backwards as the mussel suddenly came away in her hand.

She could hardly believe that she had it. She put it on the rock beside her. The task was less difficult now. There was a gap in the nest and the other shells were more accessible. She developed a method: grab with both hands, twist and pull. Some of the mussels were quite small but she didn't care. She tried to ignore the sting of salt in the cuts and grazes on her hands and fingers, concentrating instead on her growing pile of mussels.

She had twenty or more when she heard the wave coming. It was still a short distance off the point but it was big enough to frighten her. She scrambled up and slid and slipped her way across the kelp. She

Win! Win!

was past the seaweed and a good way back from the point when she heard the wave break. She looked back to see the foaming water spilling over the kelp where she'd been crouching a moment before. She scanned the spot for her mussels, but they were gone, scattered by the breaking wave that was now sucking them back into the sea.

There was still no one about on the beach. Hungry and alone, she couldn't even find the energy to cry.

In the corner beside the sofa, Sean steadied the branch of pine and put the last stone in the bucket

"Brilliant!" said Marie. "It's a great Christmas tree. Now where did we put the decorations we left here last year?"

Outside, a car drove past, tooting its horn. Sean got to the door in time to see the rear end of a red trailer disappearing down the road.

"They're here!" he shouted so loudly that Fin dropped the cracker he was gnawing and started to cry. "Sorry, Mum. I have to go. Can I leave the tree? I have to go and find Nick."

"Go!" said Marie, picking up Fin. "Away you go." She shooed him out the door. "Just don't get in the way of their unpacking."

Sean leapt through the long grass and down the dunes. The tide was coming in, but there was still enough beach left to run along the sand. He sprinted until he reached the wooden steps leading up to Nick's place and took them two at a time. Then he ran, out of breath, towards the car parked at the back of the house.

"Nick! Hey, Nick!"

"Sean!"

They stood there on the drive, grinning awkwardly at each other, hardly able to believe they were together again.

"Well, go on, give each other a hug or something," teased Kirsty.

"Leave them alone," said Julia.

Jess shook her head. "That's guys for you. How's it going anyway, Sean? How's that little brother of yours? Cute as ever, I'll bet."

"He's good," Sean said. "Fin's cool. But he's getting a couple of big back teeth."

"That's trouble," said Julia. She gave Sean a hug. "Good to see you again, Sean. I'm looking forward to catching up with your mum."

Win! Win!

"Grab that bag, Nick," called Tom from the boot. "Oh hi, Sean. How's it going?"

"After I take this inside, can I go with Sean?" begged Nick. "Please? I'll get all the firewood in when I come back."

"Away you go," said Tom. He looked at his watch. "But don't be too long. We're supposed to be getting rough weather, so we do actually want the fire going tonight."

"How rough?" asked Nick. "Too rough to fish?"

"Some heavy rain and big swells brewing, then it's supposed to clear in the morning."

"Come on," said Sean, leading the way, "before the weather packs up."

They ran along the beach and through the marram grass to the base of the tree where the hut was perched.

Nick tested the ladder. "Seems okay. Doesn't look like the wood's rotted or anything. I'm going up."

"Right behind you," said Sean.

At the top of the ladder, Nick pushed up the hatch in the floor. "Looks fine. Roof's still on, walls holding together."

"Maybe we could add another storey these holidays? I found some more iron under . . ."

"Hey! Someone's been up here! The lock on the

trunk's smashed." Nick hauled himself into the hut. "They've taken our food supplies and everything."

"Bet it was those kids at the house beside the camping ground," said Sean, poking his head up through the hatch.

"That house is still empty," Nick told him. "I saw it when we drove past."

"Well who then?"

"Dunno. But we're going to have to put a decent padlock on the latch."

Above them, a sudden gust of wind swept through the branches of the trees and a scattering of twigs clattered onto the roof of the hut.

"Weather's changing," said Sean. "Let's take a look around the village before it starts raining and see who's arrived."

"And maybe see if we can spot anything to use for our raft before someone beats us to it," added Nick.

But by the time they were back on the beach it had already started raining.

Chapter 7

Standing on the rock with dark cloud filling the sky, Phoebe knew that there was nothing else for it – she *had* to go back out to the kelp and start again. And this time she must put the mussels she collected into a container so that, if another big wave came, she could take them with her when she ran.

She peeled off her hoodie, tied knots in the ends of its sleeves, and laid it beside her. Then she went to work on the mussels.

The water was definitely rising and the sea was becoming rougher but, by the time the next big wave arrived, she had collected more than thirty mussels. She scooped them up in her hoodie and struggled over the kelp, her legs shaking with the effort, to the highest point of the platform.

Cloud had filled the sky. By the time she reached what was left of the sand, it was starting to spit with rain. She'd have to go immediately or the tide would be too high for her to return along the beach.

"Come on, Alfie, gotta go." She retrieved her jacket from the beach, but couldn't feel his weight as she lifted it. Then she saw the little shreds of orange fabric lying in the sand.

"Alfie? Alfie?" She felt for him in the pocket, but he was gone – he'd chewed his way out and disappeared.

Phoebe shook the jacket once more, but she knew he wasn't there. She looked up and down the beach. Nothing moved. Above, a gull circled on the wind. What if it had taken him … She tried not to think of that possibility. Could he have gone into the water? She didn't think so. That left the grass behind the sand. She dashed up the beach. Searching seemed hopeless; he was so small and the grass was so long.

"Alfie? Alfie?" He never came when he was called.

She scrambled around on her hands and knees, parting the grass, lifting pieces of wood that had been tossed up by the high tides.

"Alfie?"

She was so angry, but not with Alfie. It was Mick she was furious with. If it wasn't for him she wouldn't have done what she'd done, she would never have had to run away from home and Alfie

Win! Win!

wouldn't be lost. Mick didn't care about anyone but himself. How *could* Mum not see through him?

"Alfie!"

She shouted out his name, and now it was raining hard. There was no way to stop her rising panic. Alfie was so small. How far could he have gone?

Phoebe wasn't sure what made her look back at the beach – the breaking of an extra large wave, the screech of a gull – but, when she did, there he was, waddling towards her, perhaps following his own scent trail, a little scrap of dull white against the grey sand.

She ran over to him and picked him up. His tiny heart was beating even faster than her own and his back was wet.

"Alfie, don't ever do that to me again."

The wind was stronger now and Phoebe was shivering. She pulled her jacket over her head, put Alfie into the unchewed pocket and picked up the mussels. She was into the next small bay before she realised that it was too late to return along the beach.

She looked up at the bush. It couldn't be *too* difficult to go back through the trees. She'd be able to hear the sea all the way and there had to be more shelter in the forest than on the beach. She left the

sand and pushed her way through long grass and thistles and into the trees.

The shrubs formed a thick, wiry hedge so that, after a time, she realised it was actually easier to crawl under them than to try to battle through. It was difficult, inching her way forward, dragging the hoodie of mussels with her, but she couldn't leave them behind. They were all she had to eat.

It occurred to her as she tugged herself free of some vines that there was little point in returning to the village anyway. Now that she'd had to abandon the tree hut, there was nowhere to sleep, and it wasn't as if there were dry clothes waiting for her to change into. It was just that being close to the village somehow gave her a sense of security.

On the other side of the shrubs at last, she stumbled out onto clear ground. The trees above were tall and the light was draining from the sky. She rearranged the mussels in the hoodie and tied the sleeves together around her shoulders to make a rough pack.

It was five o'clock now. That left at least three hours before dark and it would never take her that long to get back to the village. She was desperately hungry. It made sense to get a fire going and it was better that she did it here, rather than closer to the settlement, where the smoke might be seen.

Phoebe dumped the hoodie back on the ground.

"Come on, Alfie," she said aloud. "Got to find some sticks. Got to build a fire."

"You two are soaking!" said Julia when the boys returned.

"Drenched!" said Marie.

The two women were sitting in the living room at Nick's place, drinking coffee and eating Christmas cake.

"Get those clothes off and get some dry ones for Sean," Julia ordered.

"Where's Fin?" asked Sean.

"Jess and Kirsty have got him upstairs, I'll bet," said Nick.

Sean followed Nick into his bedroom and caught the clothes he threw to him from a drawer. Downstairs he could hear the murmur of voices. Sean liked Nick's mum, but he didn't like it when she and Marie got together, because he knew it was Dad they'd be talking about.

Julia was the one who had finally got Mum to

make Dad move out of the house. Mum had been thinking about it for ages, but it was Julia who knew what Mum had to do to make sure that Dad wasn't allowed to come back or contact Sean or Fin without permission. Sean knew that Mum had had to do something, but it had gone on for too long. Dad was over all that stuff; he'd changed. He'd said so himself.

Sean went down to the kitchen to make toast while Nick took a shower. "I can't believe you've been on your own for eight months now," he heard Julia say from the living room. They didn't know he was there.

"I'll never go back to the way it was," said Marie.

"Has he actually said he wants to come back?"

"Oh, all the time. But it's the same old story: 'I've changed, I won't do it again, I just want to be with the kids.'"

"So you wouldn't have him back?"

"Not a show," said Marie. "I've got my job. It gives us the things we need. We can manage without him."

"What about the boys?"

"Well, it'd be nice if they could see a bit more of him. But he's got a long way to go before that can happen. A leopard can't change its spots overnight."

"Too true," said Julia.

Sean felt a lump growing in his throat. Mum hadn't told him this stuff. She'd never said that Dad wasn't coming back to live with them. He started biting at one of his nails, the way he always did when he felt worried.

"Got the toast ready?"

Nick was standing at the kitchen door, drying his hair. The rain was driving against the window, blown against the glass in big sweeps by the wind.

"That's a storm and a half," said Tom, coming into the house. "Wouldn't like to be out in a boat tonight." He sat down at the table and helped himself to the toast Sean had just made. "Now, about this raft," he began. "Have you boys sorted out what you're building?"

"We've still got a few days to go," said Nick. "And we have to find a third person to go in the triathlon with us."

"Who are we going to get?" asked Sean.

"Dunno," said Nick.

"Maybe we could go to the camping ground and see if anyone there is interested," suggested Sean.

"I'm sure you'll find someone who's looking for some fun," said Tom. "What section of the race will they have to do?"

"The running," said Sean and Nick at the same time.

"So we just have to get a guy who's a fast runner," said Sean.

"Or a girl," said Tom.

Win! Win!

Chapter 8

The rain was lashing down by the time Phoebe had collected enough twigs and sticks from beneath the trees. She assembled the little pile under the lip of a rotting log, screwed up the sheets of writing paper from the hut, which were now damp, and poked them into the kindling. Her fingers were almost too numb with cold to strike a match and, when she did, the flame was immediately extinguished by the wind. She tried again and again, until finally, hunching right over the twigs, she was able to light the paper.

It burned pathetically until the flame died. What was she going to do now? She was freezing cold and so desperate for food that she felt more light-headed than hungry. She put her hands in her pockets to warm them up and felt the candle. It was possible, she thought. It might just keep burning longer than the damp paper.

Phoebe repeated the same match-striking routine and was on her sixth attempt when the wick finally caught. She pushed the candle flame under the twigs and waited. After a few seconds, a faint trail of smoke rose from the pile, then a denser cloud. She felt a flutter of excitement and then a wave of relief as a flame finally broke through the smoke.

Little by little, she fed the fire with more twigs, then larger sticks. The log kept off the worst of the rain and she was eventually able to put on pieces of branch to increase the size of the fire.

When it was possible to leave off feeding the flames with fuel for a few minutes, Phoebe reached for the mussels. If she placed them directly on the flame, she would destroy the fire. Instead, she used a stick to rake some of the embers to one side and sat the shellfish on top of them. Then it was a case of adding more and more fuel until a good-sized blaze was actually warming her frozen hands and feet.

Phoebe couldn't believe it when she looked at her watch and saw that it was seven o'clock. She was high up enough here to look out over the trees to the sea, crashing onto the beach. The storm had shut out much of the remaining light and it was

Win! Win!

almost dark. There was no way she could return to the village now. The prospect of a long, wet night stretched out before her, but she did have the fire and, very soon, she would have food. Water would have to wait.

When she looked back at the fire, she saw that most of the mussel shells had opened and juice was pouring out of them and onto the embers. She flicked them off the heat with a stick, pulled fresh embers from the fire, and placed more mussels on top.

The feeling of hunger had returned and, with it, an aching in her stomach. Mainly, though, she felt weak, as though very soon she wouldn't have the strength to stand.

When the shells had cooled enough for her to handle, Phoebe picked them up and pulled them the rest of the way open. The flesh inside was pale orange. She scraped it out with her fingers and dropped it into her mouth. It was so good she wanted to cry; salty and moist, with a delicious smoky flavour. She didn't mind the grit and sand that came with it.

She opened another and another. After she'd swallowed eight, she started to feel a little better: still cold and wet, but not so weak.

Chapter 8

Very soon it would be completely dark and Phoebe knew that she must gather fuel for the night while there was still time to see. She went further into the forest and found dry wood. There were piles of fallen fern fronds, too, and she made trip after trip back to her campsite, arranging them in a mound under the shrubs. They would be her mattress and, when she made her bed for the night, she would pile more on top of her.

By now, the rain had stopped falling and a watery grey light hung over the sea. Phoebe had never been away from home on her own before, and now here she was sleeping outdoors in a forest, wet and hungry. But, for the moment anyway, she was too pleased with what she had achieved to feel miserable or afraid. She had found food for herself, made a fire, and now she was preparing shelter.

"Come on, Alfie, try some mussel," she said to the damp rat, but Alfie only sniffed at the shells and wouldn't touch the flesh.

"I'll find you something to eat tomorrow," she promised. "At least you haven't been working hard like I have."

It was smoky crouching over the fire and she was growing tired. She flicked the last of the shellfish off the embers. There were six of them. She thought

briefly of keeping some for breakfast, but she was too hungry. There were two that had refused to open in the heat but, determined not to let them go to waste, she found a rock and broke one open. The flesh inside came away too easily and felt slightly sticky when she touched it. The taste was different from the others she'd eaten: sharper, almost bitter. She swallowed it whole, but it made her gag and she threw the last shell into the bushes.

The wind was less fierce by the time she dragged herself over to the mound of ferns, climbed on top and pulled some fronds over her. They were dry and scratchy and seemed to offer no warmth. If she moved or rolled over, the ones on top of her slipped off. She curled into a tight ball and cupped her hand around Alfie, who was zipped into her jacket. She was scratched and bruised and wet and cold.

As the night progressed, Phoebe napped, sleeping lightly for a few minutes at a time, sometimes half an hour, before the cold woke her. Once when she woke, she found that her teeth were actually chattering. She wished for the morning to come and, with it, the sun.

When she woke for the last time that night, it was 2am. She was so stiff and uncomfortable that she knew further sleep would be impossible. Somewhere

Chapter 8

above her, a bright silver moon was weaving its way between the canopy of the forest. The storm had passed.

She struggled out of the ferns and shuffled towards the pale orange glow of the fire. Some of the large pieces of wood were still burning and she piled more fuel on top of them. Her spirits rose a little as the flames burst back into life.

It was only when she was at last beginning to get warmer that Phoebe felt the beginning of pains in her stomach. It was not the sort of pain caused by hunger and, before long, she felt as though she might be going to vomit. She swallowed the saliva gathering in her mouth as the pain in her stomach grew stronger. Pulling her knees up tightly against her chest, she rocked back and forth.

She was very hot. Sweat gathered on her brow and, suddenly, she knew she was going to vomit. She crawled a short distance away from the fire and retched violently. A moment later, she was scuttling under the trees to find a toilet patch.

She returned to the fire, but only for a few minutes before she was sick again. If only there was some water to drink. Phoebe lay curled up in front of the fire, her stomach in a tight knot of pain. She had never felt more miserable.

By 4am, she thought that the worst might be over. She had lost count of the times she had been to the toilet and she was so thirsty she felt she could have drunk the sea. Instead, she lay where she was for another hour, then crawled back through the trees and shrubs and down to the beach, where she rinsed her mouth with salty water.

The sun had almost risen and only a few clouds were hanging in the pale pink sky. There was a hint that warmth was on its way. Phoebe looked down at herself. Her hands and arms were criss-crossed with scratches and cuts and smeared with black from the fire. She pulled pieces of dried fern from her tangled hair. Her clothes were filthy and still wet, but she didn't care. It was so good to be feeling less ill, to no longer have the pain in her stomach.

She thought back to the mussels. It must have been them that had made her sick. They had tasted so good – except for the last one. It hadn't opened in the fire and she'd known as soon as she swallowed its flesh that there was something wrong with it.

She rinsed her face with sea water and, as she did, a feeling of pride washed over her. She had survived the night, alone and sick, and now it was morning and she was still alive. True, she was still hungry – and very, very thirsty – but she was alive and she had

looked after herself. Nothing could ever be as bad as this night. And, if she had survived this challenge, she could manage on her own in any conditions. She would never have to go home, back to Mum and Mick. She could take care of herself – she'd just proved it.

Win! Win!

Chapter 9

Sean woke to the shrill beeping of his mobile's alarm and reached out sleepily to turn it off before it disturbed Fin. It was 6.30am. He sat up and pulled back the curtain from the little window beside his bed. The storm had passed and the few clouds streaked across the sky were pale pink. He pulled himself out of his sleeping bag and tiptoed into the kitchen.

"Don't forget your bait. It's in the fridge."

"I thought you were asleep," said Sean.

Marie pulled her rug up to her chin. "Just dozing. You be careful out there on those rocks. Is Tom going with you?"

"Nah. Just Nick and me."

"Well keep an eye on the waves. The tide will be coming in."

"Will do," promised Sean.

He grabbed the squid pieces from the fridge and a couple of cold sausages to take with him for breakfast.

"Be back about nine," he said.

"Just in time to go to the shop and get a paper for me," mumbled Marie.

Sean collected his fishing rod and tackle bag from the porch. At the edge of the river, Nick was already waiting for him.

"Reckon we should start down by the mouth?" asked Sean when they were together.

"Sure. If there's nothing doing there, we can try out on the rocks at the end of the beach."

They walked for a few minutes in silence and then Nick said, "I reckon it was a hunter."

"The person who took the stuff from the tree hut?"

"Yeah. Someone nosing around for a deer and then they saw the hut and decided to help themselves."

"Well, we've fixed it now anyway," said Sean. "That padlock we put on the trapdoor is real strong."

"And you know what else?" said Nick. "I can smell fish!"

Phoebe sat in the first small bay past the rocks where she had spoken to the father and son cooking mussels. Above her, on the branch of an overhanging tree, her jeans swung in the gentle breeze.

It was almost 7am. She had left her campsite while the tide was still low enough to walk back via the beach. On the way, she and Alfie had drunk from a tiny stream that trickled over the rocks to the sand.

Phoebe was unsure of her next move. She dug her fingers into the crushed shell that gave the little bay a blush of pale pink. Above, seabirds she didn't recognise hovered over the water, then dived into the waves, sometimes emerging with a flash of silver clasped in their black beaks. Gulls strutted across the rock, watching her, as if she had something to offer them.

It was strange to have been so hungry last night when now, this morning, though her stomach had a hollow, empty feel to it, she wasn't desperate for food. Of course, she would have to find something to eat eventually and she had no idea how she was going to do that. She hoped a visit to the village might give her some clues.

"What are you doing, Alfie?"

A low buzzing had caught her attention and,

when she looked down to where Alfie was stretching his legs on the beach, she found he was pursuing a large black fly.

"Yuck! Leave that!" she told him.

But it was too late. He had caught the fly in his front paws and was biting into it.

"Alfie, that is so disgusting!"

She looked away and, when she glanced back, he had finished his meal and nothing but a tiny black wing remained on the sand. He stood up on his hind legs and looked at Phoebe.

"You think you're clever, finding your own food, don't you, Alf?"

She picked him up. "I suppose you are, too. That makes two of us who can fend for ourselves." She stroked his back and ran her fingers along his tail. "You're not as white as you were, you know," she said. "And your tail is dirty. We have to find ourselves a shower sometime, Alfie. A shower would be great."

Phoebe lay back against the shells and, though she had no intention of doing so, she fell sleep. When she woke, it was to the sound of voices. To her relief, Alfie was tucked in against her neck.

The sound was coming from the other side of the rocks. She jumped up and grabbed her jeans. They were only a little drier than they had been and cold

Win! Win!

to pull on. She looked at her watch. It was half past seven. She'd been asleep for half an hour.

Phoebe tucked Alfie into her jacket and walked towards the rocks. A good distance out, two boys were fishing off a point. One of them, possibly the boy she had seen at the foot of the tree hut ladder, was winding in the line on a rod that was bent double. His friend put down his own fishing rod to assist and then a long, silver fish appeared, dangling in the air.

She saw the boys hitting it and then the one who had caught it walked up the beach with the fish and put it into a plastic bag taken from their pile of gear. If he had looked up, he would have spotted her, but he returned to the fishing spot without a glance in her direction.

It occurred to Phoebe that, if she got as far as the bag without being seen, it would be very easy to pick it (and the fish) up and then duck into the trees behind the dunes. By moving back towards the village that way, she could remain unseen until she reached the houses.

Somewhere in the back of her mind she had the uncomfortable feeling that she was becoming a different person, someone who hid and stole – but someone who had no choice.

She looked out at the point. She might not be hungry now, but she knew she wouldn't stay that way for long. She marched over the rocks and jumped down onto the sand on the other side, all the time keeping her eyes on the boys, who had still not seen her. The bag was only a few metres away now, and she rehearsed in her mind what she would do. If they turned around and saw her while she was bent over it, she would say she was taking a look at their catch, that she was interested in fishing and wondered what could be caught off the rocks.

If they saw her between the beach and forest after she had picked up the bag, she would make a run for it. Maybe if she dropped it, they wouldn't follow her.

The boys were looking directly out at the water. Phoebe stooped and snatched up the fish bag. It was heavier than she expected. Then she ran, looking back over her shoulder every couple of seconds.

By the time she reached the marram grass, the boys' attention was still focused on the sea. She pushed through lupin and stumbled over driftwood. They were still busy fishing.

Now she was in the safety of the trees. She pulled aside vines and climbed over rotten logs. She kept going without looking back. Perhaps they had seen her after all and were following. She floundered through the undergrowth, afraid and excited at the same time.

When she had gone a good distance, she stopped for a moment to listen. Nothing. Only the chatter of a bird close by and the muffled sound of the ocean. She took a deep breath and opened the bag. There were *two* fish inside – one long and silver, and the other short and slimy and olive green.

For the moment, the problem of finding her next meal was solved. At last she could look around the village.

Chapter 9

Chapter 10

"How'd it go?"

Marie was sitting on the doorstep, eating breakfast with Fin, when Sean returned home along the road.

"What? Nothing biting?" she asked when she saw the look on his face.

He scowled at her. "Something bit, all right. Something big."

"Lose your tackle? Pity. Fin and I were hoping you'd bring back a fish for lunch."

"It's not fair," said Sean. He threw his rod and gear down on the ground.

"What's not fair?"

"Someone nicked our fish. We had two. I got a really big one – a blue cod. We had them in a bag further up the beach so they wouldn't get washed off if a wave came and, when we went to get them, they'd gone."

Marie screwed up her face as though she couldn't believe it. "It must have been a gull," she said.

"A gull couldn't lift something that heavy and it would have torn the bag open. We'd have seen the bits of plastic lying round."

Marie looked unconvinced.

"And besides," added Sean, "gulls don't leave footprints."

"Sure they weren't your own?"

"They came from the other direction. They led right over to the bag and then towards the dunes. Someone nicked our fish – *and* our supplies from the tree hut!"

At the edge of the forest, Phoebe tied a knot of vine around a shrub as a marker and tucked the bag of fish underneath, where it would be shaded from the sun. She took the band off her ponytail and shook out her hair, raking her fingers through it in an effort to make it look tidy. Her T-shirt and jeans were stained with mud and charcoal and her hoodie stank of mussels, even though she'd rinsed it in the sea. She looked at her filthy fingernails. What

she wanted more than anything right now was some soap and hot water.

She stepped a little way out of the trees and checked along the beach for the boys. They were still out on the rock – two specks standing on the point. Further along, her back to Phoebe, a woman was standing at the edge of the river, watching the birds on the other side of the water.

Phoebe slipped from the cover of the trees and onto the sand at the edge of the estuary. A narrow, unsealed road led away from the river and she followed it past a mowed area of grass with picnic tables and litter bins and a public toilet. When she went to investigate the toilet block, she discovered a grimy basin with a single cold water tap jutting from the concrete wall above it. She turned it on and washed her face and hands.

In the litter bins she found the remains of a picnic: a few bread crusts and some orange peel. She picked out the crusts, thought briefly about eating them, and then shoved them into her pocket for Alfie, who wriggled with excitement. That was his meals taken care of for a day or two.

She carried on up the road and along a wider stretch of tarmac that ran behind the holiday houses. They were all occupied now, with cars in most of

Win! Win!

the driveways, and cycles and canoes and barbecues spread out on the lawns. Almost no one was up yet.

Back on the main road she had followed on the morning she arrived, Phoebe turned right into unexplored territory. Half a kilometre further on, after passing several more houses, she rounded a sharp corner to find herself looking at a shop. Sandwich boards propped on the road edge advertised petrol, food and coffee and a string of neon flags fluttered above the entrance to a camping ground.

The shop was still closed but a red mail wagon was parked outside and its driver was dumping something on the deck of the building. He waved to her as he drove away.

When the vehicle was out of sight, Phoebe wandered over to see what he'd left behind. The sight of her own face staring up at her from the front page of a pile of newspapers made her head spin.

When she had recovered enough to check that no one was watching, she tore through the plastic binding and prised one of the papers free. Folding it quickly, she stuffed it under her jacket and ran back the way she'd come.

With her photo in the newspaper, it was now too risky to go back past the beach houses but, before

she reached the turn-off to the village, she noticed the entrance to an overgrown driveway. It had obviously been unused for a long time – tall grass, bracken and foxgloves grew wildly on either side, and the trees overhanging it had grown together to form a dark arch. Not even a foot track had flattened its crop of thistles and clover. Phoebe checked up and down the road, then pushed her way through the wet undergrowth.

Fifty metres in, the drive ended in what had once been a clearing; parked in one corner, camouflaged beneath overhanging trees and a tangle of springy vine, was a derelict caravan. Damp and covered with algae, it might once have been pale blue. Grass grew across its wheels and up its sides and door. The mouldy blinds on its windows were pulled down.

Phoebe sat under a tree and took out the newspaper. She hadn't been mistaken. There she was, dressed in school uniform, smiling for her class photo.

"Police Seek Missing Teenager," said the headline. She scanned the article. "Phoebe Martine Pritchard, fifteen, has been missing since the night of December 19th." She read on. The description of what she was wearing was accurate. It said that the police were appealing to anyone who had seen her to contact

Win! Win!

them. At this stage they were not seeking anyone else in connection with her disappearance. There was a plea from her mother for her to return.

Phoebe flicked through the rest of the paper. There was nothing about what she had done at the casino. She couldn't understand it. Then she realised. That sort of news – big news of national importance – would have made headlines the day after the event. It was of far more significance than a missing teenager.

She closed the paper and sat still, watching the light on the wet dandelions and the crimson heads of the thistles that were just beginning to open. A tiny soot-coloured bird with a pale yellow breast flew close to her and landed on the twig of a dead branch. What was she going to do? Where could she go? It was impossible now to walk around the village. With her face on the front page of the newspaper, anyone might recognise her.

She read her description again: "160cm tall, slight build, shoulder-length blonde hair, blue-green eyes, pierced ears . . . probably carrying her pet white rat with her." If only, thought Phoebe, she could make herself invisible.

The sun was reaching through the leaves of the trees now and beginning to warm the air. Even in

the time she had been sitting in the clearing, it had reached the caravan. Phoebe wondered if she was beginning to think like an animal – always aware of the sun, always moving to a warmer spot as it moved.

Her stomach gurgled. She *was* becoming an animal. Food and shelter were all that were important to her. That and escaping the hunters.

She went over to the caravan and found that the door was unlocked. When she looked inside, she realised why. There was nothing there that anyone would want and the vandals had already called. Tags in pink spray-paint covered the ceiling and walls and beer bottles lay on their sides on the threadbare sofas. A candle had burned through the table, cracking the gold and white plastic surface, and the floor was covered in cigarette butts.

Phoebe pulled the cords on the blinds and they shot up, letting in the light. She turned on the tap over the tiny sink and a trickle of rust-stained water dripped out. When she slid back the cupboard doors under the sink, she found a grimy stack of chipped plates, some cups and a battered frying pan. A pot and a few mismatched pieces of cutlery were in one of the drawers, along with a white-handled knife with a wide, curved blade.

Win! Win!

She checked in the wardrobe and found, tied up in a thick plastic bag, two thin brown sleeping bags and a yellowing pillow. There was also a broom and a few ragged items of clothing.

She sat at the table and took Alfie out of her pocket. He ran across the plastic tabletop, his whiskers twitching as he investigated his latest surroundings.

"Could be worse, Alfie," she said, stroking him. "Could be rats in here!"

Phoebe smiled and, at the same time, realised that she wanted to cry. But there wasn't any point in doing that. It made more sense to plan.

"Come on," she said, lifting Alfie onto her shoulder. "Let's get this sofa outside, get the sun on it. I'm not sleeping on a damp bed tonight."

She looked back at her photo in the newspaper, then at the tarnished mirror on the back of the wardrobe door.

"They say I've got shoulder-length hair," she said aloud, picking up the knife. "We can soon fix that."

Chapter 11

"Keep pumping!" said Nick. "Don't stop. I think it's going up."

"I'm not stopping!" Sean told him.

"Yep, it's definitely inflating. Here, I'll take a turn."

Sean flopped onto the grass outside Nick's house, out of breath. The tractor inner tube they'd scrounged off Mr Jenks, the farmer who owned the land on this side of the river, was slowly filling with air.

"Do you think that patch we put on it will hold?" he asked.

Nick nodded. "Just . . . have to . . . get a . . . tarpaulin," he replied in between breaths. The foot pump they were using was ancient and slow.

"And a rope to tie it onto the tube," reminded Sean.

When the tube was half full of air and still floppy, Nick took a break and sat down beside Sean.

"It's Christmas Day tomorrow," he said. "The shop will be shut. We'll have to buy the tarpaulin and rope today." He stared into space, trying to think of ways to hold everything together long enough for the raft to make the river crossing.

"What're you getting for Christmas?" Sean asked, interrupting his thoughts.

Nick shrugged. "Don't know. I asked for a surf caster, but they cost heaps. I don't think I'll get it – not unless Mum and Dad have gone halves with my nana."

Sean twisted a tuft of grass round his finger. "My dad's got me fifty bucks' worth of phone cards for my mobile."

"Cool," said Nick, but he felt uncomfortable. Sean often said stuff about his dad that didn't sound quite right. Nick had heard Mum and Dad talking about Sean's dad. Some of the things they said about him sounded really serious. Mum once told Nick that he was an alcoholic and that he sometimes stole stuff and sold it to pay for beer. He'd been in prison a couple of times, too. There was other stuff as well, but Nick didn't know too much about that. There were things that Marie said to Mum that he wasn't *allowed* to know.

"He's working for a builder," Sean continued. "He's building this big hotel that's got a couple of hundred rooms in it."

"Cool," said Nick again, but he wished Sean would stop. Sean was his best friend, but when he talked about his dad it was as if he wasn't telling the truth.

"Let's get this pumping finished and then go to the shop," he said, trying to change the subject.

"How much will a rope and tarpaulin cost?" asked Sean.

"Dad reckons about twenty bucks."

Nick recognised a flicker of worry in Sean's eyes and added quickly, "Dad's going to pay for it. He says that, if we win, we have to pay him back from our prize money!"

Sean stood up and stepped on the pump. "What's this 'if we win'," he said with a grin. "We're the best — at least we will be when we find another person for our team."

Phoebe looked at herself in the caravan's wardrobe mirror. Lying on the tabletop and on the floor about her feet were masses of blonde hair. She pulled at some wispy strands above her ear and sawed through them with the knife. It was hopelessly blunt, but the advantage was that her hair looked as though a stylist had deliberately chipped away at it with a razor to give it a spiked effect.

She put down the knife and rubbed her fingers into her scalp, pulling up tufts of hair that immediately collapsed. If only she had some wax.

There was just her fringe to go now. "May as well get rid of it all," she told Alfie, who was on the table, burrowing under the shorn hair.

She picked up her fringe and dragged the blade of the knife across it.

"There. Finished," she told the mirror.

She whipped the little silver mouse earrings from her lobes. "Finished with those, too."

She glanced down at the newspaper and read her description again. She'd have to do something about her clothes.

Phoebe picked up the plastic bag from the wardrobe and shook the contents onto the table. There was a threadbare green cotton shirt, a black singlet and a dark blue woollen jersey that was unravelling at the cuffs. Everything looked as though it was designed to fit a man. She tossed the

jersey aside – it was hopeless – though, on second thoughts, cut into pieces, it might make a good bed for Alfie. There was nothing she could do with the shirt.

She took off her T-shirt and tried on the singlet. It was so large that the neckline came almost to the bottom of her bra. She played around with it, then had an idea. Carefully, she made a cut through each of the shoulders at the seam, then tied the fabric together to shorten the straps. When she put it on again, it fitted well enough.

"Different," she murmured, turning this way and that to see herself in the mirror. "Kind of funky."

Next she took off her jeans, laid them across the table and used the knife to chew through the fabric above the knees.

"Hi, Tessa," she said to herself in the mirror, modelling her new shorts. "Where are you staying?"

"At the camping ground," she replied to herself. "My dad and I are staying in a tent. He's over from Canada for a couple of weeks."

She looked away and out the open door of the caravan to where a pigeon had just landed, shaking drops of water from a wet branch. It was *partly* true. Her dad *was* in Canada. His name was Daniel and she'd met him a few times when he'd come

back to see his parents. Phoebe didn't call them her grandparents because they lived at the other end of the country and she never saw them. Daniel worked for an oil company – or at least he did the last time she'd seen him. She tried to work out how many years ago that was and couldn't.

"Let's hang these sleeping bags out to air," she said to Alfie before she had time to feel sorry for herself. She poked him down her neck and he tucked himself in to the top of her bra.

She took the bags outside and, as she gave the first one a fierce shake, something flew out of it and landed in the long grass. When Phoebe picked it up, she discovered that it was a flat brown leather wallet. She opened it, fumbling in her eagerness to pull back the zip, and found inside a twenty-dollar note.

It was like discovering gold. It was as though her whole world had suddenly changed; as though Christmas had come a day early. Phoebe held the note in her hand, admiring it. She could go right over to the shop and buy whatever she wanted to eat. She could hardly believe it.

She undomed a little pocket and found a few coins. The wallet must have been in the caravan for a while because some of the coins were the big heavy ones that could no longer be used. But she now had twenty-four dollars altogether!

The name inside the wallet said "Dreaver" and a checkout docket with the change bore a date that was more than a year old. Had it been that long since someone visited the caravan?

Phoebe put the wallet on the table and finished shaking out the sleeping bags. By the time she'd turned them inside out and hung them on a branch in the sun, her stomach was rumbling again.

It was time to go shopping, but she couldn't leave by the exit onto the road because that might alert people to the fact that someone was staying in the caravan. Instead, she made her way, with difficulty, through the scrub that ran parallel to the road until she judged that she was a short distance past the entrance to the camping ground.

When she arrived at the shop, the bundle of newspapers had gone from the deck. Those that were left were now stacked in a neat pile on the counter inside. Quickly, Phoebe turned her back on the woman serving and looked at the shelves. She chose a loaf of bread, a jar of peanut butter and, on impulse, a bottle of orange juice. She wanted chocolate, but she knew she couldn't have it. The money had to last.

Win! Win!

A child came into the shop and took his time choosing lollies. Phoebe didn't want to stand at the counter for too long in case she was recognised, even with her new haircut, so she went to another section of the shop and discovered a shelf of personal items: combs, soap, toothpaste, shampoo and (her heart gave a leap) boxes of hair dye. There were only three colours: blonde, black and brown. She picked up the box of black and turned it over. It was fourteen dollars.

Phoebe took an anxious look over at the counter. The shopkeeper's back was turned. Quickly, she lifted her black singlet and tucked the dye down the front of her jean shorts. She'd lost weight over the last couple of days or it would never have been possible. Then she picked up a comb and a packet of soap and moved uncomfortably over to the counter. She kept her head down, pretending to look at the cover of a magazine sitting beside the newspapers. Even when she put out her hand for the change, she didn't look up.

"Thanks," she said again as she left.

Outside, leaning against a dented grey station wagon dotted with patches of priming paint, a man was smoking a cigarette. His greasy hair was too long and he needed a shave. As Phoebe passed, he

kicked at the gravel with dusty black cowboy boots and clasped the wide silver buckle on his belt. He was looking down at the ground, but he was also looking at her, she could tell.

She hurried away, walking swiftly down the road until she was out of his sight. Then she ducked into the bush and made her way back through the trees to the caravan.

Chapter 12

Phoebe had watched her mother dye her hair once. It had seemed like a complicated procedure, involving lots of anxiety about timing and wiping dye off ears and neck in case the skin was marked by the colour. But it couldn't be all that difficult. Kids at school were always streaking their hair with purple or red, or highlighting it with blonde streaks.

For a moment, Phoebe thought of school and her friend Sreya. Sreya knew what was going on in Phoebe's life – about how Mick's gambling was getting worse and worse. If Sreya had been home, Phoebe would have contacted her. But she had gone to Europe with her family for the holidays, leaving before school had finished, and she wouldn't be back until the new term started, which was weeks away.

Phoebe turned her attention back to the box of hair dye and pulled out the instructions and a pair of thin plastic gloves. There was also a tube of paste to pierce open and a bottle of pale liquid to mix with it. She felt as though she was back in her chemistry class.

She studied the instructions. Timing was everything: if you wanted your hair to be very black, you left the dye on for forty minutes; less if you wanted a lighter shade.

"What do you think, Alfie?" she asked. "Black or black-black?"

Alfie was busy licking peanut butter off a knife lying on the table and hoovering up the crumbs of bread left over from Phoebe's brunch.

"I'll need water," she said aloud, reading the instructions. She picked up the pot and went out to the rusting tank at the back of the caravan. The water she collected was murky, with a few mosquito larvae wriggling through it. She flicked them back into the tank.

Back inside the caravan, she squeezed the paste from the tube into the plastic bottle. Then she shook everything together until the mixture became a pale brown slurry.

"That's not black!" she told Alfie, studying it.

Closing her eyes, she squeezed the slurry onto her hair and began combing it through the strands.

The smell was horrible and the fumes from the dye were acrid. Her eyes were stinging now and she could see that it was distressing Alfie, too. She picked him up and took him to the other end of the caravan where the window was open and he could get fresh air.

"Don't you dare go outside!" she warned him.

By the time she had finished massaging the dye through her hair, she had it all over her face and ears. She took off the gloves, tore a piece off the green shirt to use as a sponge and cleaned herself up as best she could. She checked her watch. She would have to stay like this, with a pile of gunk on her head, for another twenty minutes.

Phoebe picked up the box and looked at the glossy black hair of the woman on the front. Outside on the road, a car slowed and tooted its horn. Phoebe wasn't very far from the road, but she felt completely safe. She was sure no one would come walking into the clearing and, if they did, she'd say it was her uncle's caravan and that she was staying in it for a while – unless it was the owners who arrived, but it seemed likely that they had long since given up on the place.

Outside, the sun was drying her T-shirt and the underclothes she'd hung up in a tree. She'd had a

wash with the soap she bought and felt almost human again. Tonight, when it was dark and she could safely light a fire without giving away her presence, she'd cook the fish. She'd boil some water, too, and use it for drinking and cleaning her teeth.

Once more, she felt a thrill of excitement. Here she was surviving, just like last night in the forest, and doing it without anyone's help.

When the twenty minutes were up, Phoebe took the pot out to the back of the caravan and began sluicing the dye from her hair. It took many scoops from the tank before the rinsing water finally ran clear, as the instructions said it must. When at last it did, she squeezed the water from her hair and rubbed it as dry as she could get it, using the shirt as a towel.

Alfie poked his nose out the caravan window, watching her. She clucked affectionately at him, then looked more closely. His white coat was blotched with black.

"Alfie!" She dropped the shirt and ran inside. "How did you get dye on you?"

And then she remembered: she had picked him up while she was wearing the gloves. The dye had come off on his coat and there was now no chance of removing it.

"Oh well, I guess that makes two of us," she said.

When the sun had almost dried her hair, she dared to look at it in the mirror. It was jet black. She put her earrings in again, studying her image, and decided that she liked it. The short, damp tufts of hair were easy enough to pull and shape with her fingers. In the black singlet and denim shorts, with her black sneakers, she thought she looked interesting, in a wild kind of way. Not at all like Phoebe Pritchard.

She felt so confident about her appearance that she decided to return for the fish before dark. She would take Alfie with her in the decaying daypack she'd found hanging underneath the tank stand.

"In you go, rat," she told him. "No chewing holes while you're in there."

She took her normal route out onto the road, and it was only when she was about to turn down the straight that led to the beach houses that she had the strange feeling that she was being watched. She looked over her shoulder. There, lying back against a rock in a field above the road, was the man she'd seen at the shop. She looked away and walked as confidently as she could towards the houses, hoping that he would think she was from one of them.

Chapter 12   97

It wasn't at all difficult to find the fish. She bundled them into the daypack and put Alfie in its outside pocket. Now that she had money to buy food, she wished she had never stolen them.

She walked back along the beach, passing a couple of girls who were playing on the sand with a little boy, helping him to decorate his sandcastle. Two women watched them from deckchairs at the bottom of the dunes.

"Hey, Finny, here's a good one," called one of the girls.

The little boy waddled over to her and took a shell from her hand. Then he ran to the castle and stuck it into the top. The women in the deckchairs applauded. Phoebe wanted to clap, too. She so wished it had been Mum in one of the chairs, watching her play with baby Jak.

A wave of homesickness washed over her. It was the first time since she'd run away that she actually ached to see him, to hold his little starfish hands and let him sit on her knee while she bounced him up and down until he grinned so much he dribbled.

"Hi," one of the girls said to her.

"Hi," said Phoebe with a smile, wondering if she'd been staring.

Further along the beach, a whole family was

busy stringing up lights through a tree outside their house. A blow-up plastic Santa wobbled in a deckchair beside them.

"Christmas," thought Phoebe. It was Christmas Eve and tomorrow everyone would be celebrating. Suddenly, she felt, not lonely, but afraid that she *might* be. What did you do on Christmas Day when you were completely by yourself? In the city, you could go to the City Mission and eat your dinner with a whole heap of lonely people, but not here, in the middle of nowhere.

She imagined being alone in the caravan, with just Alfie to share a meal of bread and peanut butter, and only the pink graffiti on the walls for decoration. It was awful and she ordered herself to stop thinking about it. If she gave way to self-pity, no matter how much she wanted, just for a minute, to wallow in it, she knew it would only make things worse. She had to be strong. She didn't have a choice.

"We'll get some chocolate," she told Alfie. "That little block that I saw in the shop."

It had only cost a couple of dollars. She would buy it when she got back and she and Alfie would share it on Christmas Day.

Chapter 13

The shop was crowded when Phoebe arrived. Campervans and cars were pulled up outside and, at one end of the building, a group of people stood on the deck, waiting their turn to use a public phone.

Phoebe jostled her way inside.

"Excuse me!" said a brisk voice behind her, and the woman who had served her that morning pushed past with a crate of milk, heading for the refrigerator.

Phoebe found the chocolate and took it to the counter. She was relieved to see that the newspapers had all gone. When the man serving her handed over her change, she watched him carefully for any sign of recognition, but he just smiled and said, "Don't eat it all at once!"

Outside on the deck, she lingered, reading the notices taped to the shop window. A carnival was advertised for the afternoon of New Year's Eve in the picnic ground next to the beach, with a bonfire to follow at night. Someone had lost their sunglasses and there was an old bath wanting a home. She was about to move away when a bright poster caught her eye.

"New Year's Day Triathlon" it announced. "Bike from the bridge to the picnic ground, raft across the river, run back along the bush track to the bridge." It went on to explain that individuals or teams of three could enter and that rafts must be built by the entrants themselves. But it wasn't the details that Phoebe was interested in, it was the prize money. The winning team received a hundred dollars. She did some quick maths: that was thirty-three dollars each if you were in a team – enough for her to live on for a week.

"It's here. They've put it up!" The boy she'd seen fishing that morning, the one with the short dark ponytail, pushed in front of her. He was holding a coil of rope and a plastic bag with something blue inside it.

"Excuse me," he said. "I just want to see this."

"Hey, a hundred dollars!" said another voice. "That's more than last year."

Now his friend was beside her, squeezing her

out of the way. The two of them pressed their noses against the window.

"Is that triathlon held *here*?" she heard herself ask.

The boys turned around at the same time.

"Yep," said the one with the rope.

"Can anyone enter?"

"Sure." Now the other one was speaking. He was pale, with very straight brown hair and a fringe that hung over his eyes. "They have it every year, don't they, Sean?"

But Sean wasn't listening. He was looking at the people milling around the car park and standing on the deck.

"There's got to be *someone* who wants to go in it with us," he said. "Hey, why don't we put an ad on the shop window?"

"What are you looking for?" asked Phoebe, though she was fairly sure she already knew.

"We need a third person for our triathlon team," said Nick. "Someone who can run."

"I can run," said Phoebe. "Fast."

"Where are you staying?" asked Sean.

"The camping ground," she answered, without hesitation. Then, almost enjoying herself, she added, "I'm Tessa."

Win! Win!

"Right. And I'm Nick and he's Sean. We'll have to talk about this. We could come round to your place. Are you in a caravan or what?"

"A tent," said Phoebe. "But we're just going out for a walk. Maybe we could meet up later."

"Sure," said Nick. "About three?"

Phoebe nodded and listened carefully as he gave instructions on how to find his house. Then she wandered towards the camping ground until the boys had disappeared up the road.

"She won't show up," said Nick. "She'll have chickened out."

He and Sean were waiting on the back lawn of Nick's house, leaning against the raft and sucking nectar from clover flowers.

"She will," said Sean.

"But what'll we do if she doesn't?"

"Hello?" A hesitant voice called from the side of the house, and the boys jumped up.

"Thought you'd come along the road," said Nick, grinning with relief at Phoebe.

"River," said Phoebe, smiling back. She looked at

the raft with its board deck, strapped firmly onto the tube. "Is that the raft for the triathlon?"

"Yep," said Sean. "What do you think?"

"It's great. Can we try it out?"

"Almost. Got to get the paddle organised first," explained Nick.

Kirsty poked her head out the kitchen window. "What's with the big meeting?" she asked.

"This is Tessa," said Nick. "She's going in the triathlon with us."

"You're from the camping ground, right?" asked Kirsty.

Phoebe nodded. It was Kirsty who had smiled at her on the beach that morning when she was watching the little boy decorating the sandcastle. But she was pretty sure Kirsty didn't remember her.

"We're having a drink on the front lawn and some early Christmas cake," said Kirsty. "Mum said to tell you all to come and have some."

After spending the last few days alone, Phoebe found it strange to be with so many people. Nick introduced his mum and dad as Julia and Tom and Julia passed her a big slab of Christmas cake. It was rich and delicious and she wished that Alfie could have some. But he was back in the caravan, safely locked inside a cupboard. Phoebe's hair might be

Win! Win!

black, but in the newspaper it had said that she had her pet rat with her. She couldn't risk being seen with him.

"Where did you say you were from?" asked Tom.

"From . . . Rider," she said, grabbing at the name of any town she could think of and realising that it was the one she thought her father lived in.

"Rider?" asked Julia.

"It's in Canada. My dad and I live in Canada," lied Phoebe, "and we've just arrived over here on holiday."

"There's a Rider in Australia," said Tom. "I was invited to a veterinary conference there once."

"You don't have a Canadian accent," said Sean.

"We've just shifted – about six months ago," explained Phoebe. "We've come back for Christmas."

"So are you visiting family here in Spratten?" asked Jess.

"Nick said she's in the camping ground, remember?" Kirsty told her.

Phoebe's face grew hot. They were confusing her with all their questions.

"What a nosy bunch you all are," said Julia, laughing. "Don't take any notice of them, Tessa."

"I like your hair," said Jess, changing the subject. "It's a great cut."

"Thanks," said Phoebe, too quickly. She squirmed uncomfortably in her deckchair.

"Cool colour, too," said Kirsty. "I have the most amazing purple-black lipstick that would look just awesome with it. Want to try it on?"

"She's here to do triathlon stuff," interrupted Nick.

"Yeah, yeah," said Jess, "but girls have got to have fun. Go and get it, Kirsty."

Nick and Sean looked really annoyed, but Phoebe was starting to enjoy herself. Nick's sisters were crazy, talking non-stop and giving the boys a hard time. She let them put the lipstick on her while Sean and Nick went off to build a paddle. When anyone asked her about herself or her family, she tried to answer confidently – but it wasn't easy.

"Did you come along the road to get here?" asked Jess. She was putting make-up on Phoebe's eyes.

"I walked along the river."

"Well, if you're on the road, just watch out for this creepy guy."

"What's all this about?" asked Julia, putting down the book she was reading.

"A real greasy-sleazy," Kirsty told her. "Jess and I were walking back from getting Dad's newspaper at the shop and he tooted at us and gave a wolf whistle."

"A wolf whistle! Do men still *do* that?"

"This one did," said Jess. "He was, like, so *ancient*."

"You mean my age," said Tom with a grin.

"Like I said, Dad, ancient."

Phoebe laughed. It seemed a long time since she'd done that. She realised that she really was having fun.

"Anyway, we saw his car again after lunch," continued Kirsty, "creeping along the road behind the houses like he was looking for someone."

"Did he have longish hair?" asked Phoebe.

"Long and greasy," said Jess.

"I think I did see him," said Phoebe.

Nick and Sean returned, wearing swimsuits.

"Ready to check out the triathlon route?" Nick asked Phoebe.

"Sure," she told them. She looked in the mirror Kirsty had handed her. "Awesome! I like it!"

"Too good for going in the water," said Jess.

"Did you bring your swimsuit?" asked Sean.

"I . . . I forgot," said Phoebe.

Kirsty jumped out of her seat. "No worries," she said. "You can wear my spare one."

When Phoebe had changed into the swimsuit and put on the life jacket Nick handed her, she and the

boys picked up the raft and headed for the river.

"Good luck," Tom called after them.

"Tessa's really nice," said Jess, watching them disappear over the dunes.

"*Really* nice," added Kirsty. "Don't you think so, Mum?"

"Very," said Julia, without looking up from her book. "Pity you can't believe a word she says."

"What?" demanded Jess and Kirsty at the same time.

"You've been a social worker for too long, Mum," said Kirsty. "You don't trust anyone. You need a holiday."

"She's having one," said Tom. "And she's dead right about that girl."

Chapter 14

"Thirteen minutes," said Nick, consulting the waterproof watch he'd got from his gran last Christmas.

"But that was with all of us hanging onto the raft," Sean pointed out.

They were standing on the beach on the other side of the river.

"I'll have a go on my own," said Nick.

Sean and Phoebe climbed a sandbank to watch.

"Where's your place?" asked Phoebe, when Nick was out on the water.

Sean pointed across the river to the tiny hut at the end of the row of houses. "It belongs to my uncle. He lets us stay in it."

"Why's it got no neighbours?" asked Phoebe. "It's all on its own."

"It's on my mum's family's land," he explained.

"All those sections between us and the next house will get built on by my cousins one day."

"What do your mum and dad do?"

"My mum looks after my little brother, plus she works part-time as a cleaner. My dad's a builder."

"So is he going to build you a beach house of your own over there sometime?"

"It's not like that," hedged Sean. "He doesn't live with us."

They looked out at the water. Nick was paddling hard, but the incoming tide was towing him off course.

"I wish he did," said Sean, after a while, "but Mum won't let him."

He didn't know why he'd said it aloud to this girl he'd only just met. He didn't talk to anyone about stuff like that, not even Nick. Maybe it was because she didn't count, because he didn't know her.

"Some people can't live together," said Phoebe. "It's not good for them."

They sat in silence, watching Nick as he struggled to reach the other side.

"Ten minutes!" he shouted back to them once he'd made it across. "I'm coming back over."

"I'll do the biking," said Sean to Phoebe. "Nick really wants to raft and I don't care which I do."

Win! Win!

For the rest of the afternoon, they worked on the running, testing out the track together and then timing Phoebe on her own.

"You'd be faster in running shoes," said Nick. "You wouldn't have to dodge the sticks and stuff."

"I'm hopeless in shoes," Phoebe lied. "I always run in bare feet."

They crossed back in the raft and, when they'd changed into their dry clothes, Sean and Phoebe set off down the road together.

"See you tomorrow," Nick called after them.

"Who are you having Christmas with?" asked Phoebe, when she and Sean were by themselves.

"Just my mum and Fin – he's my little brother."

"Not your dad?"

Sean didn't answer.

"That's okay," said Phoebe. "It's none of my business."

"He can't come," said Sean. "He's not allowed."

"Hey, there's that car again," said Phoebe. She pointed to the battered grey station wagon parked on the edge of the road a few houses away. "It's that guy Nick's sisters were telling me about."

Ahead, the vehicle's door opened and the man with the long, greasy hair got out, wearing sunglasses. He took them off and waved.

Chapter 14   111

Sean waved back and, without saying anything, sprinted off along the road.

Phoebe stayed where she was, watching as Sean reached the car and the man put his arm round his shoulders. They got into the vehicle together.

Phoebe moved to the edge of the road and sat down on the grass. Was it Sean's uncle – the one who owned the hut? Or was it his dad? After fifteen minutes, she thought she should go, but she didn't want to leave Sean on his own with the guy in the station wagon. She thought about going back to tell Nick's sisters, but what was there to say? No one had forced Sean to get in the vehicle.

Just as she was trying to decide what to do, Sean got out and went round to stand near the driver's window. He took a few steps back as the car did a U-turn and drove away down the road. After he'd watched it disappear, he looked back at Phoebe.

She walked over to him. "Was that your dad?"

Sean nodded. "You won't say anything, will you?" His voice was pleading. "It's just that, if anyone knows he's been to see me, he'll be in big trouble."

"Who would I tell?" asked Phoebe.

"My mum?" said Sean. "Nick's mum?"

"Tell me why you're not allowed to see him," said Phoebe.

Win! Win!

Sean took a deep breath and felt in his pocket for the phone card Dad had given him. It was for ten dollars, not fifty. He hadn't got his Christmas pay. There was a problem with his wages going into his new bank account.

"He's leaving Spratten now," he told Phoebe, avoiding the question. "He's going up north for the rest of the holidays and he isn't coming back. Don't you believe me?" he asked, when Phoebe didn't reply.

"Do you believe yourself?" she asked.

Back in the caravan, Phoebe took Alfie out of the cupboard and lay back on the sofa, with him on her chest. She couldn't stop thinking about Sean and what he'd said about his father. It reminded her of the way Mum talked about Mick, and it made her feel tired.

She stroked Alfie's coat, but he didn't respond by waddling up to tickle her face with his whiskers.

"What's the matter, Alfie? Are you tired, too? Maybe you didn't like being in that cupboard all by yourself?"

Chapter 14

She sat up and looked at him. Was his breathing a little too rapid? It was hard to tell. She put him on the table and offered him some peanut butter on her finger, but he only sniffed at it and wouldn't lick any off. When she gave him water, he lapped it up eagerly, but he seemed reluctant to move around.

"Are you all right, Alfie?"

She watched him for so long that she started to think she was just imagining something was wrong.

"We'll see how you are later," she said finally, cutting a tube of sleeve from the old blue jersey and putting Alfie inside it and back into the cupboard. "In you go," she said.

Much later, when it was almost dark, Phoebe went for a walk to the camping ground. Kirsty and Jess had said they'd been there the night before and that everyone had Christmas lights strung around their caravans and tents. There was a big Christmas tree in the kitchen, too, and someone had decorated it with sea shells and dried seaweed sprayed with gold paint. They said it looked fantastic. Phoebe had agreed, pretending that she'd seen it all. Now she was going to take a look.

When she reached the camping ground, there were people everywhere, sitting outside round their barbecues, and the smell of frying meat and onions made her mouth water.

Kirsty and Jess were right about the lights. They were beautiful – bright strings of illuminated colour, trailing down the sides of tents, flashing from the windows of caravans and strung through the branches of almost every tree.

Phoebe wandered around the whole place and then went to look in the kitchen and dining room. Someone had turned off the lights there and large candles were flickering on all the tables. A man and a woman, each with a guitar, were tuning up in the corner of the room.

"Carols start in fifteen minutes," said the woman, looking up at her. "Coming?"

"Maybe," said Phoebe. "Thanks."

A group of excited little children was hanging around the doors.

"When can we go inside for songs?" they asked Phoebe.

"Soon," she told them with a smile. "Just a few more minutes."

She went into the washing block next door to see what it was like. Steam and the fragrance of shampoo wafted out above a closed door and it occurred to Phoebe that she could easily come to the camp for a shower. No one would know she didn't belong here,

that she wasn't actually a camper.

She made plans for tomorrow. It would be a Christmas present to herself – a hot, early-morning shower and then the chocolate. She took a deep breath and looked at her reflection in the mirror over the hand basins. She was doing okay. She felt proud of herself – maybe not for what she had done at the casino, but certainly for what she was achieving now.

"Lucy?" A woman poked her head around the door and called out towards the shower. "Carols are starting."

"Coming," came the reply, drifting up with the steam.

The woman looked at Phoebe. "Coming carolling in the kitchen?"

"Sure," said Phoebe.

It was only on her way back home after the singing that Phoebe felt the edges of sadness creeping in. It was just something she'd have to get used to – pushing away its constant attempts to invade.

She passed the shop and looked along the deck to the phone at the other end. Just one call was all it would take to let Mum know she was safe. But what if Mick answered? She couldn't bear it – couldn't stand, even for a second, to hear that slippery, lying voice.

Win! Win!

There was another reason why she didn't want to call home, too. Somewhere in the back of her mind, though she knew that it was impossible, there was the tiniest pinprick of hope that Mum had told Mick to clear out and never come back. If Phoebe phoned home and Mick answered, then that hope was gone.

Sean didn't know how lucky he was to have a mother who was strong, who put him before anyone else. She'd wanted to tell him that, back there on the road after he'd seen his father. But she couldn't. She couldn't risk saying anything that might give her away.

She was about to cross the road towards the caravan when she heard a car approaching. She jumped into the long grass beside the ditch and crouched down as the car stopped at the entrance to the camping ground, under the big overhead light where hundreds of moths flitted through the amber glow. The driver got out, took a swig from the bottle he was holding, then threw it onto the lawn beside the shop.

Phoebe's heart beat faster. Sean had said his dad was leaving, but now he was back. Perhaps he'd never left in the first place. Should she let Sean know?

Chapter 15

Phoebe climbed out of the ditch once the car had driven into the camping ground and ran back to the caravan.

"Alfie!" she whispered. "I'm back!"

She listened for the excited scuffling he always made when he heard her voice, but there was nothing.

"Alfie?"

She lit the candle on the table and slid back the door of the cupboard. But he wasn't in the woollen sleeve of the jersey. He was lying on the bottom of the shelf, lethargic and panting too quickly. She lifted him out gently and he lay limply on her hand.

She sat down with him and stroked his back. When she offered him some water he seemed unusually interested in it, licking it from the inside of a milk bottle top for several minutes.

"Now you try going back to sleep, Alfie," she said, popping him back in the cupboard and covering him with the piece of jersey. She would check on him before she went to bed.

Outside, there was enough moonlight to see by as she assembled the sticks she had gathered earlier in the day, tucked paper under them and set fire to them with a match.

The fire was soon burning well enough to set the pan over the ashes and cook the fish. Once, on the wharf at home, she'd seen someone prepare their catch for eating and she'd done her best to copy them – slitting open the stomach of each fish and pulling out a string of gut. There was no oil to cook with, so she waited until the fish were blackened on both sides, then pulled them onto the grass and peeled off their skin.

The flesh inside was hot and pure white. She picked it up in her fingers and dropped it into her mouth, wishing she had salt to put on it. It was the first proper meal she had eaten since leaving home and it filled her in a deliciously satisfying way. She picked up a morsel and took it inside to offer Alfie, but he was lying where she had left him under the jersey, and wasn't interested.

Phoebe was worried, but there was nothing

Chapter 15

she could do tonight. In the morning, if he was worse . . . Phoebe closed the cupboard door. What *would* she do if he was worse?

She lay back on her bed with her eyes closed and suddenly it was as if a switch had been turned on in her head. It was something that Nick's father had said that afternoon – something about being invited to a veterinary conference in Australia. Did that mean he was a vet?

Maybe he was just someone who sold supplies to vets? Or worked in a vet's office? Whatever it was, he might know something about sick animals. If Alfie wasn't better in the morning, she'd take him to Nick's father. It might be a risk to be seen with a rat, but she had no choice and, besides, she now looked so different to the photo in the paper that no one would suspect anything.

But Alfie wasn't *that* sick, was he? Surely, in the morning, he would be fine.

Nick was trying out his new surf caster on the back lawn on Christmas morning when he heard the commotion. It was the girl from the camping ground, running across the grass holding something and calling out to him.

"Is your dad here?" she panted. "It's Alfie! It's my pet rat."

"What's wrong with him?" he asked, but Jess was already calling from the deck where she was standing in her pyjamas.

"What's happened, Tess?"

"It's my rat, Alfie. I think he's eaten rat poison. He's really sick."

"Dad!" screamed Jess, running back into the house. "Dad! Get out of bed! Hurry!"

"Let's see him," said Nick.

Phoebe opened the tube of jersey. Alfie was panting shallowly. His eyes were closed.

"There was something wrong with him last night, but he wasn't this bad. I think he's going to die."

"Let me see him," said Tom, running over in his boxer shorts. "Bring him inside and put him on the table."

"Dad's a vet," said Kirsty. "He'll know what to do."

"I had him in a cupboard. I think there must have been rat poison in it," said Phoebe. "I found a few crumbs of it this morning."

"When did he first have access to this poison?"

"Yesterday afternoon. When I found him last

night he was sort of limp, but not like this."

"Do you know the brand of rat poison?"

Phoebe shook her head.

"Did you bring some of it with you?"

"No." Phoebe was crying now, she couldn't stop herself. "Will he be all right?"

"I'll need a sample of that poison as soon as possible. In the meantime, I'll assume it's the usual type and I'll give him an injection of vitamin K."

"Have you got it here?" asked Phoebe.

"He always brings his stuff with him," Jess assured her.

"I'll go and get the bit of poison left in the cupboard," said Phoebe, heading for the door.

"Mum can take you," said Nick. "It'll be faster."

"No," said Phoebe. "I'll run."

"But you're out at the camping ground," argued Jess. "Let Mum drive you there."

"No, I'll go right now." She looked at Alfie lying on the table. "Look after him," she said, running out the door.

"Why didn't her dad bring her here?" asked Kirsty.

Julia came into the kitchen, tying her dressing gown round her waist. "What on earth is going on?" she asked. "How's anyone supposed to sleep in around this place?"

"It's Tessa's rat," explained Kirsty. "It's eaten rat poison. It's really sick."

"Where's Tessa?"

"She's gone to get a sample of the poison for Dad," Nick told her.

"Why didn't you get me to drive her back?"

Kirsty shrugged. "She didn't want us to. She just took off."

"I'll go down to the camping ground and meet her," said Julia. "No one will know I'm in my dressing gown." She headed for the door to the garage, then stopped. "Why didn't her father bring her along in their car?"

Phoebe ran all the way to the caravan. There was no time to take her usual back route. She ran straight down the overgrown drive and didn't care who saw her.

She reached into the cupboard and pulled out the tin that Alfie had eaten from. She should have checked before she put him in there, but the cupboard was long and narrow and it hadn't occurred to her that there was anything in it. She tipped the

poison into a piece of newspaper and folded it up.

She had reached the end of the drive and was headed out onto the road when a horn tooted. It was Julia, leaning from the window of her car. "Tessa! Over here! I've been looking for you in the camping ground – to give you a lift back."

Phoebe leapt into the car.

"What were you doing down there?" asked Julia, turning the car around and accelerating up the road.

Phoebe couldn't think of an answer to that. Instead, she held out the piece of newspaper. "I've got a sample of the poison," she said. "Do you think Alfie will be all right?"

"Tom's a very good vet," said Julia. "He's especially good with small animals."

Back at the house, Phoebe ran inside. The others were still gathered around the table where Alfie lay and he was still alive. She opened the newspaper and held out the contents for Tom to inspect.

"It *is* rat poison," he said. "Alfie will have internal bleeding, but the vitamin K injection I've given him will probably take care of that."

Phoebe gave a shaky sigh of relief.

"I haven't seen that sort of poison for quite a while," continued Tom. "I'd say it's pretty old. When did you get it?"

Win! Win!

"I can't remember," said Phoebe. "It was right in the back of a cupboard, so it could have been there for years."

"I thought you were staying in a tent?" said Jess.

"I'll make some coffee," interrupted Julia. "I think we need it. And we'll have the Christmas mince pies to go with it."

"This colour on his coat," said Tom. "What is it exactly?"

"It's hair dye," said Phoebe, feeling her face turn red.

"Hair dye?" asked Kirsty.

"My mum's," said Phoebe quickly. "She picked Alfie up when she was dying her hair and she had some of the dye on her hands."

"So does your mum live here or in Canada?" asked Jess.

"Help me with the coffee, Jess," said Julia.

"You don't need to snap, Mum," said Jess. "I was just asking if . . ."

"Stay and have a mince pie with us, Tessa," said Julia. "It'll give us all a chance to see how Alfie manages with that injection."

"Okay," agreed Phoebe. "I told my dad I might be a while."

Chapter 16

"Sure you don't want a ride back?" asked Nick, when Phoebe was ready to leave.

She shook her head. "I'm fine. I'll carry Alfie in my pocket. He likes that."

"Walk slowly," advised Tom. "The rat poison causes internal bleeding. We don't want Alfie to get bumped around."

"And I just give him some soft food when he starts to feel like it?" she asked.

Tom nodded. "By this evening he should be coming right. If not, make sure you bring him back."

"How much will all this cost?" she asked.

Tom smiled. "If your dad wants to pay for the injection, it's thirty dollars. But there's no charge for the service."

"Thanks. I'll bring the money next time I come round. Sorry I disturbed your Christmas morning."

"See you tomorrow for the triathlon training," said Nick.

"Sure," said Phoebe. "I'll be here."

"Now don't all speak at once," said Julia, holding up her hand for silence when Phoebe had gone. "It's Christmas Day and we are not going to spoil it by holding an investigation into who that girl is and what she's doing here."

"But Mum!" wailed Jess. "She's so weird! You heard what she said about her mother and the hair dye on the rat. She doesn't even *live* with her mother."

"And how can you bring a rat here on a flight from another country? You'd never get it through customs without it being quarantined for weeks," added Kirsty.

"I thought she was supposed to be staying in a tent at the camp," said Jess. "Since when do you get a cupboard in a tent – especially one that's filled with old rat poison?"

"I don't think she *is* staying at the camp," said Julia quietly.

"What?" asked Tom, packing away the last of his equipment.

"When I went to collect her just now, she was coming out of that overgrown driveway just before the shop."

"The one where Martin Dreaver used to keep his caravan?" quizzed Tom.

"Who's Martin Dreaver?" asked Jess.

"An old man who used to trap rabbits," said Tom. "He died a year or so back. His caravan might still be there, for all I know."

"That's exactly what I was thinking," said Julia.

Nick, who had said nothing since Phoebe left, stood up. "Well I don't care who she is or where she's staying! She's the third person in Sean's and my team. We've only got a few more days to go before the triathlon and we have to get training, so can you all just leave her alone?"

He stomped outside to look at the raft. What a great Christmas Day this was turning out to be. Why couldn't everyone just mind their own business!

Phoebe let the warm water trickle down her back as she soaped herself all over once more. She had washed her hair and picked out the grime from under her fingernails. She felt cleaner than she had for days.

Better yet, it was only halfway through the

morning and Alfie was improving already. He lay quietly in her shoe while she showered, opening his eyes occasionally. Outside, on the camping ground lawn, children were playing with their new Christmas toys.

Phoebe had taken Alfie back to the caravan and let him lie on the table while she took the sleeping bag off the bed and tried to make the inside of the place look unlived in again. Outside, she'd covered over the traces of her campfire. Now that Julia had seen her coming out of the driveway, there was no way she could afford to stay at the caravan – not during the day, anyway.

Phoebe turned the dial on the shower to make the water hotter and rinsed off the soap. Julia was bound to be suspicious – Nick's whole family would be. Phoebe had made a bad job of lying to them, but she'd been so upset about Alfie that she couldn't think straight. And now she had the added problem of trying to find the thirty dollars to pay Tom for the injection.

She dried herself on the remains of the cotton shirt and nibbled on the chocolate she'd bought from the shop the day before.

"I'll save some for when you're well, little rat," she whispered to Alfie, then bent down and kissed

him. "It won't be long now before you'll be feeling better."

Coming out of the washing block, Phoebe saw Sean's father emptying an armful of beer bottles into a bin beside the camp kitchen. He was also swigging from the full one still in his hand.

She completed a circuit of the camp to give anyone watching the impression that she was staying there, then went out the gate, heading for her few possessions hidden in the trees not far from the caravan. As she waited to cross the road, she spotted Sean walking towards her with Fin on his back.

"Happy Christmas!" she called out, but Sean didn't look pleased to see her.

"Hi," he said. "This is Fin."

"I know. I met him on the beach the other day. Where are you two going?"

Sean looked uncomfortable. "I'm just taking Fin for a walk while Mum cooks Christmas dinner."

"I'll come with you."

"No, it's okay." Sean scuffed at the stones on the road with his shoe. "We have to be back soon anyway."

"I know where you're going," said Phoebe.

Sean looked up at her.

"I thought you said your father was going away –

going straight away and not coming back."

"He had to stay another day. His car's got something wrong with it."

"Sure," said Phoebe. "Whatever."

"Listen," said Sean, "he wanted to see Fin, that's all. He's leaving today, after we've been to see him."

"You should be supporting your mum," said Phoebe angrily. "She's doing something really difficult. She's doing it for you and you're just going against her."

"What would you know?" Sean shot back at her. "You don't know what my father's like. He's changed. He doesn't drink any more, he's got a job and . . ."

"Yeah, yeah," said Phoebe. "And if you believe that you're as pathetic as he is. If your father's so different now, then why won't your mother have him back?"

"Mind your own business!" said Sean, pushing past her. "You don't know anything."

In the bushes well back from the caravan, Phoebe sat on the ground with Alfie sleeping in her lap. She looked at the chocolate. She was so angry with

Sean that she didn't feel like eating it any more. She stuffed it in her pocket and picked up a twig, snapping it into tiny pieces. He was so sucked in – just like her own mother!

Month after month, year after year, Mum had gone on believing that everything would come right, that next week or next payday it would be different, and that Mick would stop gambling.

"Mick, Micky, Michael, *Him*." Phoebe would never say "Dad", no matter how much her mother wanted her to. She lay back on the hard ground and stared up into the trees.

At home, they could see the High Tower Casino from their house. The whole world could see it, rising above every other building in the city, tall and grey like a rocket ready to blast off. At night, it was a bright gold laser beam, or a neon sword with an eerie, glowing purple handle.

Mick knew everything about the High Tower. He was in love with it.

"The purple part is the restaurant," he told them. "It's got a glass floor and gold walls and tables made from solid blocks of jade. The lift's made of plate glass. It gets you from road level to three hundred metres up in the restaurant in just sixty seconds."

Mick liked to talk about the waiters who brought

cocktails to the tables in glasses with frosted sugar rims.

"The most amazing thing is," he said, "if you're a VIP, like me, you're in a special part of the restaurant with your own video screen beside your table."

Phoebe didn't need him to tell her that the screen was there so that gamblers could keep an eye on the gaming tables while they ate.

Mick said there was a special gaming room, too, where only the professionals – the ones like him who knew what they were doing – got to go.

She felt sick when she thought about it. The High Tower Casino was all he'd talked about for months. He went to see it every day while it was being built, watched every TV item about it, followed its progress in the newspaper.

At the start, he'd pretended it was the architecture he was interested in. "Futuristic" was what they called it, he said. The architects were from New York. Two helicopters would work for three weeks to lift the restaurant into place. He went on and on about it.

On a still day, when it was sometimes possible to hear the helicopters at work, Mick would stand outside listening to them. Inside, making dinner, Mum would watch him. Phoebe could see the

fear in her eyes, but Mum wouldn't say a word against him.

"He's only interested in the architecture," she'd say. "All that other stuff, it's behind him now."

Phoebe closed her eyes, remembering the night she'd gone by bus to the casino with the can of paint in her bag. It had been hot and humid. The city was holding its breath, waiting for rain.

It hadn't been difficult to find the foyer where the mayor had cut the ribbon just a few weeks before, officially opening the city's first casino in time for the festive season. He had made a speech, admiring the pure wool carpet with its hand-woven map of the city's harbour and praising the artworks on display.

Mick had been there, too. When he came home that night, on a high from winning two hundred dollars (he'd probably lost four times that amount), all he could talk about was the artwork in the foyer. Most of all he raved on and on about the Binyani sculpture. It was a masterpiece, he said, the most wonderful, priceless work of art, and the casino had bought it for the whole city to enjoy. It was called "The Luck" and it symbolised what the casino was all about. Mick said it *was* the casino. He insisted they all go on a trip to see it.

It was Mum's meek agreement that had made Phoebe so angry – that and the fact that she had dared to agree on Phoebe's behalf to anything Mick suggested. But it was her anger, in the end, that had allowed Phoebe to do what she'd done. With fury seething inside her, she had grown strangely calm, and the calmness had allowed her to plan. It had made her determined, methodical, unwavering.

A few nights later, she was outside the tower, walking into the foyer of the casino. Amazingly, the reception desk had been unattended and there were only two other people waiting there. There was no mistaking the Binyani sculpture. At home Mick had attached a newspaper photo of it to the fridge door with a magnet.

She had walked over to the silk cord that kept back the public and taken out the test pot of orange paint – specially chosen because it was oil-based and unlikely to be removable. Calmly, she had unscrewed the lid. Her anger had gone by then, but her resolve was strong. She felt intensely calm, almost numb.

She had raised her arm, balancing the paint pot in her hand and taking great care, for some ridiculous reason, not to spill a drop on the carpet. She was about to throw it when she heard someone shouting

at her. She looked back at the man standing at the swing door behind the reception desk and, just as he began running towards her, she'd thrown the paint at the sculpture and fled.

There had been no time to watch it hit, but she distinctly remembered the gasps of the onlookers and the fright in the eyes of the man behind the desk. She had fled out the door and into the street. It was raining and the footpath was shining purple and red from the neon lights of the tower.

Chapter 17

Sean's father may have been telling the truth when he told Sean that he'd leave as soon as he'd seen Fin. Walking around the camping ground on the afternoon of Christmas Day, Phoebe was unable to find his car. She checked again, just before six, and he was still not there.

She sat on the deck of the shop and stroked Alfie. He stirred in her pocket and repositioned himself into a tight ball. She clucked to him, a sound he liked to hear. He had been moving more since the middle of the afternoon and there was no doubt he was recovering. Behind Phoebe, a couple from a campervan was using the phone.

"No rooms left at that place," she heard the woman say in what sounded like a French accent. "Give me some more coins and I'll try the other number."

Phoebe listened to the coins falling into the slot. Then she heard one of them drop onto the deck.

"Oh no!" said the woman. "It's gone down between the boards!"

"It's okay," said the man. "I've got another one."

Phoebe sat where she was. If one coin had dropped through the deck, how many more were under there?

She waited until they had made their phone call and left, then got down on her hands and knees. The front of the deck was boarded up, but it was open at both ends and there was reasonable light under there. She took off her hoodie and hung it on a nail from the corner post of the shop so that Alfie would be safely out of the way of any passing cats or dogs. Then she lay down on her front and eased herself under the deck.

It was dusty and dry on the ground, and she tried not to think about spiders. With just enough room to move, as long as she didn't try to crawl, she dragged herself a few metres along – and reached her first find. It was a tarnished two-dollar coin. She saw another after that, then found two fifty-cent pieces. It was like striking gold – like being in a mine that had never been tapped. Above her, feet thumped across the deck. Someone called out to a child and the footsteps disappeared.

Win! Win!

By the time she was halfway along the ground under the deck, the pocket of her shorts was bulging, but when she reached the far end, directly below the phone, she almost gasped aloud. There were coins everywhere. She stuffed as many as she could down the front of her bra and closed her fists around the rest.

When Phoebe pulled herself out from under the deck, she was covered in dust and dirt. She grabbed her hoodie and darted across the road, back to her bush hideaway. There she lay the hoodie on the ground and spread the coins out on it. She was ridiculously excited as she sorted them into piles. It was like playing banks. She counted the treasure, then counted it again – and discovered that she had collected fifty-two dollars!

She put aside thirty for Alfie's injection and scooped up the rest. It was enough to buy food for at least another week, and perhaps she could get something other than peanut butter to go on her bread. She lay back, dreaming of sausages and eggs and all the other treats she would buy herself when the shop opened the next day.

"They still haven't found that teenager, you know," tut-tutted Marie. She went missing on the 19th of December and now it's the 30th."

Marie was reading the newspaper in the kitchen while Sean worked on Nick's bike – the one he was riding in the triathlon. "Her parents must be out of their minds with worry."

"What's that?" asked Sean, his mouth full of toast.

"That fifteen-year-old girl who's gone missing," said Marie. "They haven't seen her since before Christmas."

"Mmm." Sean wasn't really concentrating. He gently wrestled the bike pump from Fin's hand. "Leave that alone, Finny," he coaxed. "I need it."

"How's the training going?" asked Marie, putting down her newspaper.

"Great," said Sean. "We've put in four solid days of training since Christmas. I reckon we've got a good chance of winning. Tessa's a really fast runner."

"She must have plenty of energy, if what she eats is anything to go by," said Marie.

"Yeah, she does eat a lot," agreed Sean.

Every time Tessa came around to his place and Mum offered her something to eat, she almost grabbed it off the plate – and she always had more than one of whatever there was. Mum said she didn't

140   *Win! Win!*

mind, but when it was chocolate biscuits or cake –
the sort of thing that they didn't have very often –
Sean wished Tessa wouldn't take so much.

Sean had to admit that he liked Tessa, even though
she should have minded her own business about his
taking Fin to see Dad on Christmas Day. But at least
she hadn't mentioned it in front of Mum.

What was strange about Tessa, though, was that
she never asked Nick or him back to her place. She
always had an excuse. Sometimes she said that her
father was asleep and that they'd disturb him if they
came round to the tent. At other times she said that
he was away for a walk and she wasn't allowed to
have friends around when there was no one else at
their campsite. It didn't make sense, but Sean never
said anything to her. After what had happened on
Christmas Day, he didn't talk to her about anything
much except the triathlon.

"Come here, Fin," said Mum.

She picked him up and pulled him onto her knee.

"Why don't you and I read one of your books
and leave Seanie to get on with his mending?"

"Boop, boop!" said Fin.

Sean looked up from his pumping. Mum was so
relaxed. He couldn't remember a time when he'd
seen her so happy. He felt really guilty about what

he'd done on Christmas Day. It had been a disaster anyway. The moment he saw Dad at the camping ground, he knew that he'd been drinking again. He could smell the beer on his breath when he hugged him and Fin and the inside of the car had stunk of alcohol. Dad didn't even have a tent. He'd slept in the back of the wagon.

Sean had waited for Dad to give Fin the present that he'd said he had for him, but he didn't give him anything. And, after a while, it didn't even seem as though he wanted them to stay. He told them he had a long way to go that day and that he'd better be on his way. Sean had hardly had time to get Fin into his daypack before Dad was driving off.

As he left the camping ground and turned onto the main road, Sean could see that he was already drinking out of a bottle. For the rest of the day, it was as if he was only pretending to enjoy Christmas.

"Hello?" called a voice outside the hut.

Sean looked up as Tessa came into the room.

"You're early," said Marie. "What's your dad up to today?"

"Just the usual," said Phoebe with a shy smile. "Reading, listening to music."

"Would you like some toast? We're just having breakfast."

142   *Win! Win!*

Phoebe looked at her watch. It was only nine o'clock. It was hard not to come round to Sean or Nick's too early, but she always woke before seven in the caravan and then she was in a hurry to move out and into the trees in case anyone came down the driveway. It made the morning seem very long.

"Toast? Okay, thanks. I'll make it myself."

Phoebe liked it at Sean's place. She especially liked his mother. Being at Nick's was okay, too, but his mother and father sometimes asked questions that made her feel uncomfortable – as if they might suspect something. She had to be careful what she said around them. Marie didn't ask much at all. She just seemed happy to talk about holiday stuff, like how warm the water was or what Fin had done at the beach.

Fin had abandoned his book, so Marie picked up the newspaper again. "There's a girl missing," she said. "Phoebe Pritchard."

Phoebe's heart missed a beat.

"It's been in the paper all week," continued Marie. "At first the police thought she'd just run away from home but now they think they might be dealing with a homicide."

"They think she's been *murdered*?" asked Phoebe.

"That's what it says," said Marie. "I suppose, if

she did run away from home and hitched a ride somewhere, well, anyone could have picked her up. She's only fifteen."

"Aren't you going to eat your toast?" asked Sean, standing up with the wheel in his hand.

Phoebe's mouth was dry. She spread apricot jam over the toast, but she couldn't take a bite. What must Mum be thinking? Every day she would be waiting for news and there would be none. Even though she wasn't going home, Phoebe now knew that she had to let Mum know she was safe. But how could she contact her?

"Just because she hasn't contacted anyone, it doesn't necessarily mean she's been murdered," said Phoebe. "I mean, she might not want to be found and, if she contacted someone, then that would give her away, wouldn't it?"

"How do you mean?" asked Marie.

"Well, if you phone someone, the call can be traced."

Marie put the newspaper down and reached for her cup of tea. "I don't think so – not if it's very brief. I saw something about it on a TV programme once."

"Really?" asked Phoebe.

"I'm sure I'm right," said Marie. "It was only

Win! Win!

a TV programme, but I've read the same thing somewhere, too."

"Are you coming?" asked Sean.

"Okay," replied Phoebe vaguely. "Marie, is it all right if I leave Alfie with you again? He really likes it in that old birdcage you found in the shed."

"Absolutely," said Marie with a smile. "Fin loves watching him. Have a good time training and, if I'm not here when you call back for Alfie, I'll see you at the carnival tomorrow."

Phoebe picked up the toast and made herself take a bite as she followed Sean along the beach to Nick's.

Chapter 18

"Your girlfriend is here, Nick," teased Jess, looking out the window. "You'd better hide the Christmas cake."

"Why does she always arrive so early?" asked Kirsty.

"So she's got time to eat?"

"That is quite enough, Jess," said Julia, pouring herself some more coffee. "Tessa's very welcome here. I enjoy her."

Jess snorted. "You were the one who said you couldn't believe a word she said!"

"*And* went sneaking down to that old caravan of what's his name's to see if she was living there," added Kirsty.

"That was days ago," said Julia. "And she wasn't living in the caravan, was she? So I was wrong." She took a sip of her coffee. "I have to admit that Tessa *is* a different sort of girl but, in fact, I like her very much."

"Quit talking about her," warned Kirsty. "She's almost here."

Nick was tired of hearing his sisters going on about Tessa. And as for Mum and Dad, they were always asking her too many questions. Best to keep her away from them if he could.

"Hi," said Nick, when Phoebe and Sean came inside. "I'll just grab the life jackets and we can go."

"Want a piece of toast, Tessa?" asked Jess.

"No thanks. I just had some at Sean's."

"Let's go!" said Nick. "You take the paddle, Tessa."

At the edge of the river, they pushed the raft into the water and Sean held on behind and kicked while Nick paddled himself and Phoebe across. On the other side, Nick prepared to press the timer on his watch.

"Ready, Tessa?" he asked, as Phoebe took up her position on the track.

She nodded.

"Okay, go!"

She took off, lifting her knees high as she sprinted over the leafy track, dodging tree roots and the small hollows and bumps that she'd come to know so well over the last few days. She tried to do what she always did when she was running the track – to imagine the prize money being handed to her, then

going to the shop with her share to buy a big pottle of hot chips and a bottle of sparkling fruit juice. She'd pay for the hair dye she'd nicked, too. She could just leave the money on the counter. But today Phoebe couldn't conjure up the images so easily, not after what Marie had told her. What if Mum really did think that Phoebe had been murdered?

Phoebe tried to concentrate on moving faster, but her mind kept wandering back to it. There was a huge part of her that said Mum deserved to be worried. It made up for all the times she'd put Mick first: handing over money to him that was meant for Phoebe's school trips or birthdays, giving in to him when he came crawling to her, saying that she'd have to pay his share of the power out of her own salary just this once.

Mum was weak, pathetically weak. But did that mean she had to suffer as much as she would be now?

"You've got to stop thinking about home," said a voice in her head. "You're on your own now."

Suddenly, she started running really hard. The trees became a blur as she sped past them and she could feel the wind in her short hair.

Harder, harder, she told herself. You've got to win. You've got to win!

Win! Win!

At the far end of the track, where it came out onto an area of mown grass close to the road bridge, Phoebe ran down to the beach and waved so that Nick would see her and press the stop button on his watch. She wondered what her time was – not as good as usual, she guessed. She'd had too much on her mind.

She sat down to wait for the boys to come along the track and her mind went back to home. Why couldn't Mum be like Marie? She'd done what was needed to get Sean's dad out of their lives. She wouldn't put up with his drinking any more. But what was it that had finally made her decide to send him away – that's what Phoebe wanted to know.

She had a suspicion. It was because of something Marie had said one day when she was reading the newspaper. The article had been about a woman who'd been beaten up and robbed while she was waiting for a bus. Marie had said that anyone who hit a woman – who hit anyone, for that matter – couldn't expect a second chance. It was too risky for everyone else to have them around.

It wasn't so much what she'd said that Phoebe had noticed, it was the way she said it, as though she knew what it was like to have faced that sort of violence.

Chapter 18

The spluttering of an engine drew Phoebe's attention to the road but, by the time she'd turned round, the vehicle was already on the bridge. It stopped halfway over and she saw that it was a grey station wagon. The driver got out and leaned over the railings, shaking the ash from his cigarette into the water below. Phoebe gasped. He was back. Even at this distance, she was certain that it was Sean's dad.

The sound of the boys' voices drew her attention to the entrance to the track. Nick and Sean were just emerging from the trees. The engine spluttered again and, when she looked back at the bridge, the wagon was moving off in the direction of the village.

"Five minutes thirty-three seconds," called Nick. "What went wrong?"

"I tripped," lied Phoebe. "You know I can do it in five-five."

"Want to give it another go?" asked Sean.

"Sure," she told them. "Why not?"

At eleven-thirty, they decided to call it quits. Phoebe had still not beaten her best time, but Sean was

Win! Win!

making up for it with his cycling and Nick was confident that he could knock a few seconds off the raft trip once he had some competition to challenge him.

"Are you going to the carnival tomorrow?" he asked Phoebe. "It starts at midday with a barbecue."

"Is the food free?" she asked hopefully.

"I think it costs a dollar for a sausage and bread."

"What else happens at it?" she wanted to know.

"They have a big dig on the beach," said Sean. "You pay two dollars and then you dig in the sand for containers. If you find one with a number in it, you win a prize."

"What sort of prize?"

"Chocolate mostly," said Nick. "It's fun."

"Plus they have races and a sand sculpture competition," added Sean.

Nick offered to go back to the raft and paddle it home, which left Phoebe and Sean to walk back from the bridge along the road. Phoebe wondered whether she should tell Sean about having seen his father but, after what had happened on Christmas Day, she didn't want to. Sean had to work that stuff out for himself. It was Marie she was worried

about. Marie should know that Sean's dad was in the village.

They passed the shop and the entrance to the camping ground, but the grey station wagon wasn't around. If she did tell Marie what was going on, thought Phoebe, then Sean would find out and there would be a huge scene. Maybe he would even refuse to go in the triathlon – and where would that leave her and Nick? Without the prize money, that's where, thought Phoebe. No, if she was going to tell Marie, it would have to be after the race.

When they reached Sean's place, the hut was empty. Marie had left a note on the table to say that she and Fin were at the beach.

"I'll see you tomorrow at the carnival," said Phoebe when she'd collected Alfie from the birdcage.

"I still think we should be having a training run tomorrow morning," said Sean. "The race is the next day."

"Well I agree with Nick," Phoebe told him. "A rest tomorrow means we'll have extra energy on the day."

"Okay. See you," he said. "I'm going to help Nick pull up the raft."

Alfie was as high as a kite as Phoebe carried him along the road. He raced up and down the inside of her sleeve like a battery-powered toy.

"You've been eating too many chocolate biscuits," she told him. "I saw them lying on the bottom of the birdcage. Fin gave them to you, didn't he?"

Alfie poked his nose out the top of Phoebe's T-shirt, then climbed onto her shoulder.

"Your teeth will fall out, fat rat," she said, tucking him under her shirt again.

The holiday houses were filled with people sitting on their decks or on the lawn under umbrellas. She recognised almost everyone now. Some people even made a point of saying hello to her or waving. She'd been in the village not much more than a week and already it felt like home, like a place where she belonged.

Out at sea, the water was a brilliant blue. Since the night she'd camped in the bush after collecting the mussels, it hadn't rained once. She had enough food to eat, money to buy more, and a place to sleep at night. Sometimes she felt lonely, but it was never for very long. She had

Sean and Nick to hang out with and she really liked Marie.

The only real problem was Mum. Phoebe took a deep breath and let it out slowly. She *had* to let her know that she was okay.

At the shop, she looked at the telephone. Maybe it *would* be all right to call home, just for a few seconds. She'd just say, "Hi, it's me, Phoebe. I'm fine. But I'm not coming back." Then she'd put the phone down before Mum had time to say anything. The police wouldn't be able to trace a call as short as that.

She walked down the road and turned into the bushes. She'd think some more about it.

Chapter 19

Phoebe woke that night to the sound of an owl calling close to the caravan. Alfie could hear it, too, and he moved restlessly in the bottom of the sleeping bag. She looked at her watch and saw that it was 3am. Outside, the stars were intensely bright and a new moon was lying on its back in a pool of soft yellow haze.

At home, baby Jak would be asleep, his thumb in his mouth and his toys lying beside his pillow. She missed him so much. She didn't care whether she saw Mum any more, she really, truly didn't. She'd searched inside herself, wanting there to be something that linked them together in some caring sort of way, but there wasn't anything.

That was what was so hard to accept: that she actually didn't care if she ever saw Mum again. She *had* cared about her before Mick had come to live with them, but that was so long ago now, it didn't count any more.

So, in the end, she was doing what Marie had done about Sean's dad, thought Phoebe. But she couldn't make Mick go away, so *she* had left instead.

She lay on her back and looked up at the graffiti on the ceiling of the caravan. What she'd done at the High Tower Casino, that was wrong. She had done it out of anger and frustration, because she hated Mick and it had seemed the only way to get at him. And she had run away because of it. One day she was going to have to face the consequences of what she'd done. There was no use pretending it wasn't going to happen. She couldn't hide from the police forever.

But what she had decided now, about Mum, was different and quite separate from that. She was not going to go back to live with her, no matter what happened. If she had the choice between going into a home for kids or going back to live with Mum, she'd choose the home. Maybe, one day, if Mum got rid of Mick, and if she had the guts to *stay* away from him, maybe then Phoebe might go back to her. But it was too soon to think about that.

A trickle of something wet ran down the side of her face and onto the woollen jersey she was using

Win! Win!

for a pillow, and Phoebe realised that she was crying. It was hard and lonely to admit to herself that Mum didn't love her. But it was true. Love wasn't just about *saying* you loved someone; it was about caring for them, putting them first, being there for them, being reliable. Mum wasn't doing any of that for Phoebe.

She reached down in the sleeping bag for Alfie. She felt more alone than she had ever felt in her life. Her body ached with a deep sadness and, when she tried to breathe, her chest hurt. How was it even possible to live when you were this sad? How did you manage to get up in the morning and make breakfast and go for a walk, or talk to people, or run in a triathlon?

Then it occurred to her, as it had on the night she had slept in the bush in the rain: though she was totally alone, she was also strong and able to look after herself. And she knew that she would never, ever hurt anyone in the way Mum had hurt her.

Phoebe closed her eyes and caught Alfie as he tried to scuttle past. She held him tight. Tomorrow, before she went to the carnival, she would make the phone call. She would ring Mum, tell her she was okay and say goodbye.

The smell of frying onions wafted through the picnic ground and a crowd had already gathered at the barbecue by the time Nick arrived at the carnival the next morning. He looked around for Sean or Tessa but couldn't see them.

"Too greasy," said Jess, coming towards him with a sausage wrapped in bread. "Tomato sauce is good though."

Nick caught a shred of onion that was about to fall. "Greasy's great!" he said. "Have you seen Sean or Tessa?"

Jess shook her head. "I'm going to get my ticket for the big dig. Don't eat too many sausages."

Nick lined up at the barbecue. Where *was* Sean? They were supposed to meet at a quarter to twelve and it was five past already.

When Phoebe arrived at the shop on her way to the carnival, it was just after midday and the car park was deserted.

Win! Win!

"Quiet, isn't it?" said the woman behind the counter as Phoebe stepped onto the deck. "Everyone's at the barbecue."

"Oh, right," said Phoebe.

She walked along the deck to the phone and began reading the dialling instructions. Slowly, she picked up the receiver, then replaced it. She needed a minute to think.

She headed into the camping ground and found it as quiet as the shop. Sean's father's car wasn't there. Either he hadn't stayed or he'd stayed and gone again.

She turned back to the shop and felt in her pocket for the dollar coins – part of her collection from under the deck. This was it. She was going to make the call. She'd put it off all morning. Now she couldn't put it off any longer.

There was no one on the deck as she approached the phone. The receiver, when she lifted it, felt heavy and cold. She pushed the coins into the slot and began punching in the familiar numbers. Halfway through, she stopped, then started again. The dial tone seemed a million miles away.

"Hello?"

It was Mum. She sounded tired. There was no energy in her voice.

Phoebe swallowed hard. "It's me, Phoebe," she said flatly.

There was the sound of a strangled gasp on the other end of the line. "Phoebe! Are you all right? Where are you?"

"I'm fine. I'm okay. But I'm not coming back."

She knew she should hang up, in case the call was being traced.

"Just tell me where . . ."

"I'm fine."

She replaced the handle in its cradle and looked behind her. The deck was still empty, but the world had changed. It was a different place. She was on her own and, soon, she would make another phone call. It would be to the police. She would tell them that it was she who had vandalised the Binyani sculpture at the High Tower. She would tell them where they could find her. But not before the triathlon. She had to keep her promise to Nick and Sean. If you cared about people, about friends, it was important to keep promises.

As Phoebe walked down the steps from the shop, she realised that she was very hungry. She hadn't eaten breakfast and now she was starving. Nick had said there were sausages and bread at the carnival barbecue, which was exactly where she was going.

The tide would be out so she could walk along the sand. That was one of the things that was so nice about this place that had become her home. The tide gave a pattern to the day. It dictated whether you should walk on the beach or the road, when you fished or swam or collected mussels. It was something constant that you could rely on, something that kept operating smoothly no matter what else was going on.

Phoebe walked through the camping ground again and down the short path to the wooden steps that led onto the beach. Nick and Sean would be at the carnival by now, stuffing themselves on bread and sausages.

"You can have some sausage," she told Alfie, who was poking his nose out of her shirt.

Phoebe didn't mind taking him around the village now. It didn't matter who saw him, because no one suspected that she was the missing teenager. She'd made too good a job of her disguise.

Not far ahead, Sean's hut, painted rust red, sat in its grassy paddock a good distance away from its neighbours.

"Actually, Alfie," said Phoebe, "you might be a nuisance at the carnival. I think I'll put you in the birdcage at Sean's. I'll bring you back some sausage, I promise."

She headed across the beach from the water's edge and, at the bottom of the dunes, started up the track that led to Sean's. The lupins were in full flower. In the week and a half that she'd been in Spratten, they had turned the dunes completely yellow.

For a moment, Phoebe thought she heard someone call out. She stopped to listen, then carried on. But there it was again; shouting, then a high-pitched scream. She ran to the top of the dunes and heard raised voices and angry shouting. It was coming from Sean's place, where a battered grey station wagon was parked on the road outside the hut.

"Stop it! Stop it!"

That was Sean's voice, Phoebe was sure of it.

She ran across the grass. The door to the hut was open and, inside, something terrible was happening.

Win! Win!

Chapter 20

"Get out! Get out of this house!"

Marie stood with her back against the bench while Sean's father towered over her.

"Leave her alone, Dad!" screamed Sean. "Please! Leave her!"

He ran forward and grabbed his father around the waist to pull him back, but it took just one swing from the big man's arm to send Sean crashing back against the table.

Phoebe rushed inside to help Sean up and, as she did so, Marie began pushing Sean's father away.

"You're drunk!" she yelled at him. "You're always drunk!"

He raised a fist.

"Hit me and you know where you'll end up. Now get out! Out!"

"I'm not going anywhere," he said, his speech

slurred. "Not without my boy."

He moved unsteadily towards the closed bedroom door, but Marie was there before him, planting her back against it.

"He's asleep, Dad!" yelled Sean.

"Then wake him up!"

"You leave him. Leave Fin where he is!" shouted Marie.

"Don't take Fin! Dad! Don't!" Sean was crying now, screaming and crying at the same time.

Phoebe didn't know what to do, whether to run to Nick's for help or to call the neighbours. She rushed to the door, but the holiday house across the field looked deserted and too far away for anyone there to hear her if she called. Behind her, Marie and Sean were struggling to keep Sean's father from opening Fin's door.

Suddenly, she heard Fin crying. She looked along the side of the hut and saw that the window to the bedroom was open. She dashed towards it and lifted its latch so that it opened wide.

"Fin," she called gently. "Fin, come to Tessa. Come on. I've got a surprise for you."

On the other side of the door, the shouting and banging was growing louder. The handle of the door rattled. Fin stopped his crying momentarily,

Win! Win!

then started again. If only she could climb through the window, but it was too high up. If Fin would come just a little bit closer, she'd be able to grab him and haul him through.

Something crashed to the ground in the other room. Someone swore and Phoebe heard Marie scream.

"I've got Alfie," said Phoebe suddenly. "Come and see Alfie, Fin, come on."

She pulled Alfie out from under her shirt and, as she sat him on the window ledge, she could see the little boy's face break into a smile.

"Come on," coaxed Phoebe over the noise. "Come and see Alfie."

Fin clambered out of his own bed and climbed onto Sean's. The moment he was standing up, Phoebe grabbed him by the straps of his overalls. It took all her strength, but she had him and was pulling him up and onto the window ledge.

"Come on, Finny," she said, swinging him out the window. "I'll take you for a horsy ride."

"Mouse," said Fin.

"After. Play with Alfie after."

As soon as he was in her arms, she raced with him over the grass towards the road. She was still in the field, but almost at the next house, when she

heard Sean's father shouting drunkenly from the door of the hut.

"Thass my boy you got, kid!" he called out, beginning to run after her.

"Hold tight, Fin," breathed Phoebe. "Hold tight!"

As her feet hit the road, she could hear Sean shouting to his father to stop. Phoebe kept running. Only a few more houses to go and she'd be at Nick's. They had to be home, they had to be! But, before she had even reached their drive, she heard a wailing siren behind her.

She looked back. A police car had stopped in the middle of the road and an officer was running after Sean's father. She watched the two of them struggle and, the next minute, Sean's dad was thrown to the ground. The officer driving the car ran to assist and she watched as they pulled Sean's father's hands behind his back.

Sean was with them now, bending over his father, but Phoebe couldn't see Marie anywhere. What if he'd hurt her? What if she was lying in the hut injured?

She hugged Fin tight and began walking back towards the police car.

"Tessa?"

Behind her, Tom stood on the road, trying to

catch his breath. Then Nick appeared out of their driveway.

"What's going on?" he asked. "We heard the siren."

"It's Sean's father," she said, her voice shaking. "He tried to take Fin, but I got him out of the bedroom window and ran with him and . . . I can't see Marie anywhere. She was in the house. He . . . he might have hurt her."

Tom sprinted towards the hut.

"I'll get Mum," said Nick, running in the other direction.

When Phoebe reached the police car, Sean had his face close to the ground, beside his father's.

"Dad?" he kept saying. "Dad? Are you all right? Dad?"

"Who are you?" asked one of the officers, looking at Phoebe.

"I'm a friend of the family," she said. "This is Fin. He's Sean's brother. That man," she pointed a toe at the ground, "he was trying to take Fin away."

Sean's father had been pulled up from the ground and bundled into the police car by the time Tom arrived back with his arm around Marie. She was holding a hand to her cheek.

"Give him to me. Please give Fin to me," she said,

taking him from Phoebe. "Thank you, Tessa, thank you for taking him away. You're a good girl." She put her arm around Phoebe and hugged her tight. "You're a good girl."

Sean was peering at his father through the closed window of the police car. "Dad?" he called out between sobs. "Dad? Talk to me. I'm sorry. I'm sorry, Dad."

"What's going on?" Julia was puffing from her run up the dunes. She put an arm around Marie. "Are you all right?"

"We're fine now. We're all fine."

"She's got a cut to her face," said Tom.

"Who called the police?" asked Nick.

"We weren't called," explained the officer. "We just happened to be here on another matter. We're looking for a missing girl – we think she's staying somewhere around here."

"I've got to get Alfie!" said Phoebe suddenly. "I left him on the window ledge when I grabbed Fin. He might have run away."

She dashed back to the hut before anyone had a chance to speak and, once on the far side, out of sight of the others, she headed in a straight line for the beach. There was no time to look for Alfie. If she ran as hard as she could, she'd be at the camping ground steps before the police realised who she might be and came looking for her.

At the end of the beach she looked over her shoulder. Nick was waving to her to come back, but she kept going, racing up the track, through the tents and caravans, and past the shop into the forest on the other side of the road. She grabbed the sleeping bag and her small bundle of food and pushed her way further into the trees. Any minute now and they'd come looking for her. Perhaps they'd have a whole team of searchers tracking her down.

She stopped for a moment to listen, but there was only the sound of crickets chirping and a breeze stirring the leaves above her head. What she needed was to find a place where she could think and plan. She *would* give herself up to the police, she'd decided that already. But it had to be in her own time because, first, she had to run the triathlon. No matter what happened, she was going to do it.

Chapter 20

Chapter 21

"Do you think they're right? Do you think Tessa really is Phoebe Pritchard?" asked Kirsty.

Nick stared straight ahead, trying to figure it out. "I thought she was staying with her father in the camping ground," he said.

"But we never actually saw him, did we?" said Sean. "And she *has* got a rat."

"Well, actually, it's you who's got the rat now, Seanie," said Jess, plonking herself down on a seat beside them. "You found him down the side of your bed, remember?"

They were sitting in the living room of Nick's house while, in the bedroom next door, Tom and Julia attended to Marie's cut cheek.

"If Tessa hasn't got anything to hide, she'd have come back for Alfie by now," mumbled Sean. "So she *must* be that Phoebe what's-her-name."

"Jess? Kirsty?" called Julia, opening the door to the bedroom. "Put the kettle on and make some coffee, please."

"He'll go to prison," Sean told Nick when the girls had gone into the kitchen. "They told him last time that, if he came round to our place again, that's what would happen. And he didn't just come inside. There was all that other stuff."

Nick wriggled uncomfortably in his seat. "You can visit people in prison," he said.

"I know," said Sean. "If you want to."

Later, after the adults had drunk their coffee and Sean and Fin and Marie had gone home, Nick and his family sat around the table talking and looking at the photo of Phoebe that the police had emailed through on Tom's laptop.

"How come the police figured out that this Phoebe girl is around here?" asked Kirsty.

"She made a phone call to her home about midday," said Tom. "They traced it to the coin phone at the shop."

"They got here pretty smartly," said Julia.

"There was a police car already in the area," explained Tom. "The officers were on their way to the carnival to supervise the raffle draws."

"If Tessa *is* Phoebe Pritchard," said Kirsty, "she's

a long way from home. I mean, how did she manage to travel more than five hundred kilometres?"

"I don't think there's any doubt that it's her," said Tom. He looked at the photo again. "It'd be easy enough for her to cut her hair."

"Pretty good trick to dye it," said Jess. "When she said about the rat getting dye on it when her mother was colouring her hair, I never thought about it being her *own* hair that she'd dyed black."

"You're very quiet, Nick," said Julia. "Sean's all right, you know. So's Marie. She's a very brave woman."

"We won't be able to go in the triathlon," said Nick. "All that training and it was for nothing."

"I'll run in Tessa's place," offered Jess.

"You can't," said Nick. "You're over sixteen."

"Can't you enter with just the two of you?" asked Kirsty. "Sean can cycle and you can raft and run."

"Yeah, that's what we're gonna have to do," said Nick. "But we won't have a show of winning. Not if we don't have a fresh person for the running."

"Are the police going to search around here for Tessa – I mean Phoebe?" asked Kirsty. "Or will she have gone by now?"

"They say they'll keep looking for her around the village," said Tom. "But, if she's in the bush and

doesn't want to be found, there won't be a hope of locating her."

"What I'd like to know," said Julia, "is why she ran away from home in the first place."

Phoebe's wristwatch alarm woke her just after midnight. She'd been so tired after dragging herself into the bush as far as she could go, without getting lost, that she knew she'd never wake before morning unless she set it.

She wriggled out of her sleeping bag and stretched. The moon was bright enough to see by and, in the distance, she could hear the ocean. She followed the rough track she had made the evening before until she was out of the bush and standing just opposite the shop. The tide was in. She would have to risk walking along the road.

Phoebe hugged the edge of the path, ready to dive into the trees at the side if she heard a car, but there were none. She turned down the road that led to the holiday houses and saw the roof of Sean's hut, gleaming in the moonlight. Out at sea, the water was a flat silver plate.

Chapter 21

Phoebe walked quietly along the side of the hut to Sean's window and tapped lightly on the glass. No response. She tapped again, a little louder, and the curtain twitched back.

"Tessa?" hissed Sean, when he'd opened the window.

"Shh!" she whispered, holding a finger to her lips. "Have you got Alfie? Is he okay?"

"He's fine. He's in the birdcage."

"Are *you* all right?"

"Sort of. Listen, thanks for what you did – for taking Fin away."

"Sean, I'm going to be in the triathlon tomorrow."

"But the police are looking for you. *Aren't* they?"

"You mean, am I Phoebe Pritchard? Of course I am, but I'm not going to let you down about the triathlon."

"It's okay. Nick's going to do the run now, as well as the rafting."

"No, *I'm* going to do the run," whispered Phoebe. "I said I would and I will. I'll be hiding over the other side. When Nick arrives, I'll be there to meet him, just like we practised, and I'll run to the bridge."

Sean nodded. "Then what?"

"Can you keep Alfie for me for a while, just until I can have him back?"

Win! Win!

"What do you mean?"

"I've done something really terrible, Sean," she said. "Nothing violent, nothing like that. I'd never hurt anyone. But I'm in serious trouble and I don't think that I'm going to be allowed a rat where they're going to put me. I'll phone the police and arrange to meet them after we've won the triathlon. Then I'll be going away from here. I'll be put in a home for kids who've broken the law. So can you look after Alfie for me? Please?"

"I promise," said Sean. "But can't you tell me what you've done?"

"I don't want to talk about it," said Phoebe. "I'll see you tomorrow. Don't tell anyone I'm going in the triathlon, not even Nick."

"I *have* to tell Nick," pleaded Sean.

"No," said Phoebe. "Just trust me. I've got everything planned."

"It was you who stole our stuff from the tree hut, wasn't it?"

Phoebe nodded. "And your fish. I'm really sorry. I was hungry."

"That's okay. Don't worry about it."

She stood there, leaning on the window ledge in the dark.

"What is it?" asked Sean.

"You have to look after your mum," said Phoebe. "You do, Sean. You have to forget about your dad. He only cares about himself. It's your mum who *really* loves you."

She slipped away before he had time to reply, around the side of the hut and into the darkness.

Sean closed the window softly behind her and sat on the edge of his bed. He stayed there for what seemed like a long time. In the other bed, Fin's chubby arms were spread out across his pillow and he was making soft snoring noises. Sean stood up and quietly opened the door to the kitchen.

"Mum?" he whispered. "Mum? Are you awake?"

"What's the matter?" Marie turned over sleepily on her sofa bed. "What time is it?"

"It's almost one o'clock. There's nothing wrong. Well, not really."

"What is it then?"

He sat on the edge of her bed. "There's something I have to tell you. Something I'm really sorry about."

Marie sat up. "Is this something to do with Dad?"

Sean nodded. "He phoned, just before Christmas, one night when you were away cleaning. He wanted to know . . . to know where we were going for the holidays."

"And you told him?"

He nodded again. It was too hard to speak. The words stuck in his throat. "What happened today is my fault and I'm really, really sorry."

Marie reached out for his hand. "No, it's *not* your fault," she said. "It's *his*. I know what he's like, the way he makes you tell him things."

"But not any more," said Sean in a fierce whisper. "Not any more, Mum. Because I've made up my mind. I'm not going to see Dad again and I'm not going to talk to him. Not until he's . . ." He searched for the right word.

"Until he's better?" asked Marie.

Sean nodded. "Not until he's properly better. Because what I want is to look after you and Finny."

He started to cry then. He couldn't help it.

"We'll look after each other," said Marie, hugging him tight. "That's the best way."

It was one o'clock when Phoebe arrived back at the shop after visiting Sean. A pale blue security light cast a gloomy glow over the interior of the building and moths were battering themselves against the

window. She walked along the deck to the phone and picked up the receiver. In the dim light, she read from the panel of calling instructions the contact details for the local police. Then she punched in the numbers.

"This is Phoebe Pritchard," she said clearly, when her call was answered. "You're looking for me. Tomorrow afternoon, at two-thirty, I'll be at the walking track that starts at the Spratten river bridge. I'll meet you there."

"We can pick you up now," said the voice at the other end of the phone.

"No! I mean, no thank you."

"Where are you?"

"I'll be at the bridge at two-thirty tomorrow," she repeated.

She hung up and ran across the road into the trees.

Chapter 22

"I figured out where our fish went to," said Nick the next day.

It was half an hour until the start of the triathlon and he and Sean were sitting on Nick's lawn, making a last-minute check on the bike's tyre pressure.

"I was thinking about it in bed last night," he continued. "I'll bet it was her – Tessa . . . I mean Phoebe. I'll bet she nicked them. *And* the stuff from the tree hut."

"Probably," said Sean. "I suppose she was hungry." He felt weird keeping secrets from Nick.

"It wasn't fair saying she'd go in the triathlon with us," continued Nick. "She must have known the police would find her before long."

"Yeah." Sean put on the bike helmet.

"Almost on your way?" asked Julia, coming out of the house. "Dad and the girls and I are going to see you off from the bridge, Sean, and then we'll wait up at the end of the track to watch Nick finish the race."

"I'll head off now," said Sean. "Mum and Fin are already up there." He gave Nick a high five. "Go hard!" he said.

"You, too," Nick told him.

"Don't give up, Nick," said Julia, when Sean was on his way. "Do your best and you never know what might happen."

"With only two in our team?" muttered Nick. "I can take a pretty good guess."

Phoebe was in position long before any of the other competitors. She had woken at five, eaten a couple of slices of bread and set out along the walking track before it was properly light. At the spot above the river where Nick would beach the raft, she hid herself well back in the trees.

It was a long wait for the triathlon to begin. She listened to the birds and the roar of the sea, ate the last of her food, wondered a lot about how Alfie was getting along and tried not to

Win! Win!

think about what would happen when the race was over.

Just before two o'clock, she heard the babble of the other runners and caught glimpses of them through the shrubs as they assembled at the beach entrance to the walking track. A few minutes later, the sharp crack of a starting pistol rang out from the direction of the bridge.

Phoebe retied her shoelaces and imagined Sean pedalling hard, leaning into the corner where the main road turned off into the village, dodging the potholes outside his house, then racing towards Nick's driveway and down the slope to the picnic ground.

As the minutes ticked by, the runners' chatter grew louder and they began to move towards the dunes to watch the approach of the rafts. Phoebe wanted to watch, too, but she waited until she heard the cheering begin. As it intensified, she pushed her way through the shrubs and onto the track.

If anyone recognised her, they showed no sign of it. They were all too busy calling to their team-mates on the water. From her position at the back of the group, she stole a glance at the rafts. There were all sorts: some made from drums, others from big plastic containers. A couple of them looked like piles

of driftwood logs and someone was even paddling an old bathtub with outriggers on each side.

Nick's raft was by far the most professional-looking craft, but, though he was three-quarters of the way across the river, he was being beaten by what looked like an inflatable armchair.

"Go, Nick! Go, Nick!" she screamed over the top of the other runners.

On the far side of the river, she spotted Sean, leaping into the air.

The armchair beached first, but Nick was right behind it, stepping into the knee-deep water to drag the raft onto the sand. The armchair's paddler was first to the start of the track, slapping the hand of her team-mate to set him running, but Nick was right behind her, bounding up the sand dune and almost crashing into Phoebe.

There was no time for him to say anything, not even to look surprised. He slapped her hand and, as she tore off down the track behind the lead runner, she could hear him cheering behind her.

Phoebe wasn't sure why, but she had been expecting to run against a girl. Now a muscly, long-legged boy was in front of her, pounding down the track beneath the dim tunnel of trees, and she

Win! Win!

had to catch him. Behind her, a third runner was approaching and Phoebe found herself running even harder. She lifted her knees high. She was gaining – very slowly, but she was doing it.

The track took a bend. Phoebe knew it well. If she could stake a place on the inside of the curve, it would give her the advantage. She was right on the lead runner's heels now. She could hear him breathing hard as she edged her way in against the bend, forcing him out into the middle of the track. Suddenly, she was moving ahead.

There was no stopping her now. The air rushed against her face, her heart pumped, her feet thumped against the soft earth. Soon, the final straight came into sight. Somewhere in front of her, she heard people cheering, the light grew brighter and, suddenly, the sky above was blue and she was running over mown grass and through a line of plastic, neon tape.

As she flopped onto the ground, someone slapped her hard on the back and she heard Sean's voice close to her ear.

"We did it! *You* did it, Tessa. We won!"

Except she wasn't Tessa, she was Phoebe and, for her, the race was over.

"Phoebe Pritchard?"

She nodded as the woman in the police uniform knelt on the ground beside her.

"That's me," she replied, when she had her breath back again.

"Can't she stay?" pleaded Sean. "Just till we get the cup and the prize money?"

"I'm Amy Booth," continued the woman, ignoring Sean. "I'm from Youth Aid. I've got your mother here with me."

Phoebe looked up. Her mother was standing a little way off, beside Nick's mum. She was holding baby Jak and she looked tired and thin, as though she might break into little pieces if Phoebe spoke to her.

"Please?" begged Sean. "Please don't make her go yet."

"We won! We won, didn't we!" Nick pushed through the group gathered around Phoebe and stopped when he saw the Youth Aid officer.

"Tessa?" he asked. "What's happening?"

"We're going back to our place," said Julia, coming forward. "It'll be another hour before the prizes are given out. I'm sure Phoebe will still be here then." She looked at the officer.

"I'm sure that will be the case," said Amy.

Win! Win!

In the back of the police car, Phoebe sat quietly, looking at Jak as he gurgled in his car seat between her and her mum.

"I didn't know if you were alive or dead," her mother said at last. Her voice was unsteady. "That was the worst part, Phoebe. The not knowing."

Phoebe rubbed her thumb over the back of Jak's smooth fist and noticed the roughness of her own hands.

Survivor's hands, she thought. Strong hands because I've looked after myself.

"It went on for days," continued her mother. She started to cry quietly, the tears rolling down her cheeks. "Every morning I thought, 'She'll phone today. She'll contact me,' but there was nothing."

Jak was pointing out the window and making baby noises.

"He's seen the gulls," said Phoebe as a flock flew up from their perch on the bridge railings.

"Please talk to me, Phoebe."

Phoebe shook her head.

"Take the first turn past the shop," said Julia from the front of the car. She was sitting next to Amy.

"We're the second to last house on the left."

"Phoebe?" asked her mum. "Why won't you talk to me?"

"Because we don't belong together any more." Phoebe bit the inside of her cheek hard to stop herself crying. She mustn't cry.

"What do you mean?"

Phoebe leaned close to baby Jak. He was playing with his seat belt, dribbling onto the collar of his shirt. She loved him so much and soon they would take her away from him.

"Right," said Amy, turning the car into Nick's drive. "We're going inside to have a chat, Phoebe. Just you and your mother and me."

"You can have the living room," said Julia. "I'll make sure you're not disturbed."

Chapter 23

The meeting at Nick's house was not how Phoebe had imagined it would be. For a start, Amy Booth almost seemed to be on her side, though, as she explained very clearly to her and her mum, it wasn't her job to judge anyone. But the Youth Aid officer was, Phoebe decided, very much in control of the situation.

Phoebe wanted to talk about what had happened at the High Tower Casino, but Amy said that they already knew. It had all been captured on the casino's security camera. Phoebe wanted to know what the police would do with her, but Amy Booth said they would talk about that later.

"What we need to discuss now," she said, looking from Phoebe to her mother, is why you did what you did, Phoebe. That's the really important thing, isn't it?"

On the floor, Jak lay on his back, sucking a plastic aeroplane. Phoebe's mother shifted uncomfortably in her chair.

"It was because of him," said Phoebe at last.

"Him?"

Phoebe looked out the window. You could see almost to the horizon from Nick's living room.

"Mick," she said. She looked at Mum. "And because *she* doesn't want me any more."

"Phoebe, that's not true!"

"Please, Mrs Pritchard, don't interrupt," said Amy. "Carry on, Phoebe."

When Phoebe began speaking again, everything came spilling out – all the things she had thought about for the last twelve days, for the last year, for so long she couldn't even remember any more. It was like string unravelling from a ball. And what was so terrible was that, when she had finished, and Amy Booth said that it was Mum's turn to speak, Mum said that it was all true.

"She's right. There's nothing Phoebe's said that isn't exactly how it is. I haven't been a good mother, I know that."

"Gambling addictions wreck whole families," said Amy Booth. "It may not seem like it to you, Phoebe, but I think your mother has been through

Win! Win!

as much as you have over these last few years."

"That's no excuse for the way I've treated Phoebe," said Mum. "I should have got help and I didn't." She stopped and drew in a deep breath. "But one thing *has* changed," she said fiercely. "He's gone, Phoebe. Mick has gone."

Phoebe's eyes flicked towards her mother. She tried to read the expression on her face. It wasn't what Mum had just said that was important, it was what she said next that mattered. What she said next could make all the difference in the world. Had Mick left because he had chosen to, or had Mum made him go?

Phoebe waited. Somewhere in the living room, a clock ticked loudly, but time seemed to have stopped still.

"I told him to leave," said Mum. She reached down for Jak and pulled him close. "I made him go. All those things he said about taking Jak away, I knew it wasn't true. It was just my excuse for not being brave. Mick can't take Jak away from us."

"He's gone *forever*?" asked Phoebe. "You won't let him come back?"

Mum nodded. "He's never going to change. I know that now. But *I* have. I'm stronger, Phoebe. I've got people around me who understand what

it's like to live with a gambling addict. People who will help me *stay* strong. I want you to come home, Phoebe. Please say you'll come home."

It was scary. Scary to want to go home. Scary to know that she couldn't.

"They won't let me," said Phoebe. She looked at Amy Booth. "Will they? The police will put me in a kids' home. That sculpture at the casino, it was worth thousands of dollars. And I wrecked it with that paint I threw."

"No, Phoebe," said Amy. "You didn't wreck anything. A patch of carpet was all you destroyed and it's already been repaired."

"But . . ." Phoebe didn't understand.

Amy smiled faintly. "You're not as good a shot as you think you are."

"You mean the paint didn't hit the sculpture?"

Amy shook her head. "Nowhere near it."

"Really?"

"Really."

"So . . . what will happen to me now?"

"What will happen is that you and your mum will spend time talking to a counsellor – someone who'll help you learn to be a family again."

Phoebe looked at Jak. "Just Mum and me and Jak, not Mick?"

Amy shook her head. "Not Mick." She looked at her watch. "Why don't we finish this discussion later. The prize-giving is at three. You don't want to miss it, Phoebe."

At the picnic ground, a crowd had gathered around a truck. A man who Phoebe had sometimes seen serving in the shop climbed onto its deck and spoke through a loud hailer. Phoebe stood at the back of the group, beside her mother and Jak and Amy.

The man told them that the Spratten Beach Shop was proud to sponsor the triathlon, and that this year the race had attracted a record number of entries. The spectators clapped.

"As usual," he continued, "the rafts were out-standing, though I'd have to say that this is the first time we've had an inflatable armchair entered in that particular section of the event!" He waited until everyone had finished laughing, then held up a wooden trophy covered in silver crests.

"And now for the moment you've all been waiting for. This year's winners of the Spratten Triathlon

Trophy, and a cheque for one hundred dollars, are 'Three Friends'."

"I didn't even know that's what we were called," said Phoebe.

"Off you go," said her mother. "Go up and get your trophy."

Phoebe looked at her. She seemed almost happy. Or at least as if, one day, she might be.

Nick and Sean were already on the deck of the truck when Phoebe got there. They reached down and pulled her up beside them.

On the ground below, Nick's family stood beside Marie and Fin. Phoebe waved to them all. Then she waved to baby Jak and Mum.

"The winners," said the man from the store, as he handed the trophy to Phoebe.

"Maybe you could be in our team next year?" suggested Nick over the noise of the applause.

"Could you?" begged Sean. "Could you be here for the next triathlon?"

Phoebe laughed. "I don't know," she said. "It's a long way from home."